I0548240

BEYOND THE DOOR

VOLUME 1: SUPERNATURAL ANTHOLOGY

SERENA B. MILLER   A. B. ALVAREZ

DEREK E. MILLER   JESSE R. LYLE

LJ EMORY
PUBLISHING

Beyond the Door Volume 1: Supernatural Anthology Copyright ©
2018 L. J. Emory Publishing

Published by L. J. Emory Publishing

Cover and Layout copyright © 2018 L. J. Emory Publishing

Cover & Interior design by Jacob Miller, L. J. Emory Publishing

ISBN: 978-1-940283-40-1

ISBN: 978-1-940283-41-8 (eBook)

FOREWORD

Serena B. Miller:
What happens when four writers spend a brainstorming weekend together and one challenges the others to a Word War?

A.B. Alvarez:
So, four writers walked into a bar...
Okay, four writers walked into an abandoned farm house...
Well, really, four writers walked into a well-furnished spacious farmhouse thinking they were going to be spending some quiet time together and share war stories. No bartender, but plenty of jokes.
Or maybe the joke's on us: we gathered together at a rather large dining room table, set a clock like we

were going to play chess and instead challenged each other to write in a genre none of us had ever written in with a single ground rule: for three 30-minute periods we would write like we were being held hostage by our keyboards and the ransom was the best short stories we could squeeze out of our stressed-out and anxious brains.

Derek E. Miller:

And by bar he meant coffee bar because with Word Wars you want caffeine to get an edge! The Word Wars had to be real words of a story. I was quickly told I could not type *Ha Ha Ha Ha* because they did not count as four words. Mother of pearl! They were taking my dirty tricks of battle away from me!

Jesse R. Lyle:

With so much caffeine coursing through our blood, I'm not sure how we managed to put two intelligible words together, let alone full stories.

Serena B. Miller:

For the uninitiated, a Word War involves choosing a random topic, setting a timer, and seeing who can produce the most (coherent) words in the time allotted. To stretch ourselves even further, we chose at random a genre none of us had ever written in-The Supernatural.

A.B. Alvarez:
What could go wrong?

Derek E. Miller:
Most importantly, what could go *write?*

Jesse R. Lyle:
Very *punny* Derek…

Serena B. Miller:
Writing outside my genre, and doing so in short-story form, was a challenge, but we all enjoyed the novelty of it.

Derek E. Miller:
She makes it sound quant and nice like a unicorn would come running out of the woods to the farm house to eat a sugar cube. This was Word War! The trash talk, the stink eye, the click of the keyboards might as well have been machine gun fire at each other.

Jesse R. Lyle:

I still have nervous twitches anytime I hear an overly aggressive typist hammering away at their keyboard. Looking at you *Alvarez*...

Serena B. Miller:

The quality of the twelve short stories that began to evolve in our feverish desire to out-type one another surprised us. In fact, we were so pleased with what we had produced, we decided to bundle our stories together and present it to our readers as an example of what can happen in a very short amount of time-especially when friends challenge one another to go beyond what they thought they could do.

A.B. Alvarez:

(Wait...we're all friends?)

Derek E. Miller:

When the smoke of battle cleared from our keyboards one of us would be the first to say "our number". There would be groans of disappointment and shock and awe at the word count of our opponent. We would then high five the winner of that battle and have excited talk of where our stories were going. There were protests for sure when I did my best Pee Wee Herman victory dance after I won one of the battles. It was said my dancing was a crime against humanity.

A.B. Alvarez:
Even this foreword was written by the four of us in a sort of Borg-like fervor to make sure we were in sync with each other and with the supernatural muses we called upon to assist us in our rather interesting endeavor.

Jesse R. Lyle:
I was kidnapped and forced to participate. My only hope of escaping was to win the competition. Sadly I ended up having to suffer through Derek's victory dance, Serena's feigned bashfulness, and Alvarez's nonchalant smugness as they each won and left me in the dust with their word count.

Serena B. Miller:
In addition to my own stories, we have those written by:
A.B. Alvarez, author of the techno-thriller trilogy: *Kidnapping Anna.*
Derek E. Miller, author of several young adult novels: *The Attic Diary, The Kamikaze Diary,* and *The Ghost Army*

Diary, along with his new series of short stories of *Espresso Shorts*.

Jesse R. Lyle, a promising young author, who will be publishing here for the first time.

A.B. Alvarez:

In the twelve supernatural stories of this collection you will find ghosts, an archeologist, an Amish woman, robots, fire with a deadly purpose, and avenging angels (and that's just six of the stories!).

Derek E. Miller:

Being handed the stories that were created at this epic farmhouse event was like receiving birthday or holiday gifts.

A.B. Alvarez:

Only with blood all over them.

Derek E. Miller:

The level of creativity, original thought, and the road they led me down was nothing I expected.

A.B. Alvarez:

And by the end of it all you might even find the twelve Easter eggs.

Jesse R. Lyle:

Help me escape, please.

A.B. Alvarez:

Or just tell us what you think!

Jesse R. Lyle:

Email freethejesse@ljemory.com with suggestions on how I can escape for a chance to win a free Kidnapped Jesse Action Figure, complete with miniature coffee mug and laptop.

Serena B. Miller:

Or email us at beyondthedoor@ljemory.com. We'd love to hear what you think of the first volume of Beyond the Door.

MY NAME IS SETH

SERENA B. MILLER

Whatever happened to the angels who saved Lot's family? Well one of them is still around...

My name is Seth. I do not know how old I am. Nor do I know where I came from. All I know is that I have always been. Time does not exist in the dimension where my immortal body lives.

The lack of time is a difficult concept for mortals to understand. After all, time is not real, at least not like matter is real. It cannot be touched or seen or tasted, and yet, I watch it take up a ridiculously large space in human lives. Amazing really, how they diligently watch their clock inventions as the things click away second after second as their planet slowly runs down like a wind-up toy.

I know this planet better than I want to. It is often a dark place. I am always relieved to finish my objective and go home.

My first assignment was nearly four thousand mortal years ago when I was told to save the life of a sorry excuse of a man named Lot. It made no sense to me at the time, nor to my companion, Michael, but we have learned the wisdom of doing what we are told without question.

Things went well at first. Lot was quite hospitable. He fed us and made certain the dust was washed from our feet. Then the visit turned ugly. An unfortunate problem for us, sometimes, is that our mortal bodies are very beautiful. Because of that, some of the men of the city developed a ravenous desire to "know" us. They demanded Lot send us out to them. Instead, Lot did the unthinkable. He offered up his virgin daughters in our place.

This was so unnecessary. We could have easily defended ourselves-but Lot's pride was at stake. Apparently he believed that his male guests were a much greater priority than his daughters. We managed to extricate that family in the nick of time, but I never understood why any of that experience was necessary. Especially considering what happened in the cave later.

Lot was a disgusting man, and his daughters weren't much better. The Maker had plans in place to use them, though, and so we finished the assignment and got out of there as fast as possible.

It is not easy to move between the two plains of mortal versus immortal. When I am mortal, in addition to experiencing the feelings of thirst and hunger. I have to deal with the unpleasant necessity of eliminating the fuel that I eat. I often feel physical pain. Unless I discipline myself severely, I also wrestle with the inconvenience of having mortal emotions.

Sometimes mortal women fall in love with us— again, our mortal bodies are very beautiful. This can become awkward since women are strictly forbidden to us. When I am here, I avoid mortal women as much as possible. In the past, they have never been a temptation.

The food we eat, however, is almost worth the bother of stepping into this earth dimension. Leeks and melons, roasted meats, and the delightful taste of freshly baked bread are a weakness. I am not allowed to participate in gluttony, of course, but I have to admit that while I am in my mortal body, I enjoy the tastes and textures of earth-grown food.

Lot's family were not the only people Michael and I have been sent to rescue down through the ages. There was a child who almost died from wounds incurred during a train wreck. He had an excellent surgeon, however, and a miraculous recovery. His parents were very grateful. No one noticed when I slipped away, although they talked about the mysterious doctor who performed the surgery for many years. I still do not know why it was necessary to save only that one child when some of the other children who were hurt on that train died from their injuries, but this is not something I am allowed to question.

I have been sent to keep people afloat during ship disasters, and to keep them alive during natural disasters. When there are heroic rescues but no one can find the hero, quite often that is me. I am never told why a particular spiraling plane is chosen for me to save, but I know it is important to the fabric of this world, so again, I do not question.

Unfortunately, this last time I was sent, I found it surprisingly hard to accept my immortal body again. That which I believed impossible, happened to me. I fell in love. It was wrong, and it was dangerous, but the woman was so extraordinary I could not help myself.

The biggest problem with becoming mortal is that one is forced to become truly and completely mortal. Usually after a few days, I am more than ready to be back inside my immortal body again. This time I lingered, for no other reason than I became fascinated with her.

I saw her for the first time in an orphanage in Beijing. It was not a well-run orphanage, and she was not an employee. Instead, she was a young woman who had simply felt the need to help. I was there on an easy assignment. It was a job too small for Michael to bother with accompanying me. I intended to accomplish my mission and leave as soon as possible, but once I saw her, I no longer wanted to leave.

She was beautiful in ways I had never seen in all the centuries of my mortal experience. It was not so much her physical appearance, which was stunning, but it was the expression on her face as she cradled a damaged infant. This mortal woman caught my attention, interrupted the focus on my assignment, and caused me to become somewhat emotionally unbalanced. Why? Hers was a joy so profound it hurt my eyes.

Falling in love with a mortal had never been a problem in the past. I was barely aware it was happening until it was there. Full blown passion had flared in an instant and there was nothing I could do about it.

Let me correct that. There was nothing I *wanted* to do about it.

I stood in the shadows and admired the graceful curve of her neck, the lovely lines of her face, and the tenderness with which she held the infant. She was sitting cross-legged on a shabby bed while she rocked the baby back and forth. The song she sang was a children's song—something about a little girl receiving seven diamonds. Hers was not a voice for a large stage, nor for a performance, but I was mesmerized. As I watched, and listened, I found myself growing obsessed.

By the time she finished her song and glanced up, I was standing by the bed, fighting a desire to touch her face and make certain she was real. She must have seen that desire in my face, along with my confusion, and yet there was no fear. She gazed up at me with total trust, smiled and said, "Do you want to hold the baby?"

I could have cared less about the baby. This infant was not an assignment of mine, but the woman was already holding him out to me as though she knew I would want to.

I took the child, sleepy from the bottle she had

been feeding it, warm in my arms. She stood up, smoothed back the infant's downy hair and planted a kiss on its tiny forehead. As she did so, her arm brushed mine and at that moment of touch, I could see into her soul.

I cannot read minds from afar. I have not been given that gift, but if I am touched by someone, I am often able to read their life force and see beyond the surface to the past and present, but never their future.

I have inadvertently seen such blackness in people's souls. Such dark thoughts. I had been touched by a suicide, two murderers, and a despot so cruel he did not deserve to live. I had been touched by innocent children with lives barely formed, by people bowed down by great sorrow, and by many foolish women.

But I had never been touched by someone for whom peering into their life force was like looking into clear, pure water. I knew her name in an instant. Diana. I saw her home in North Dakota and her worried adoptive mother waiting to hear from her daughter. I saw the earthbound farmer who had helped raise her and I saw her sweet and unselfish dreams.

I have not known many mortals whom I believe are worth the value the Maker gives them, but Diana was different. The beauty she carried within her was so rare I wanted to shield her from all the darkness in this world. I wanted to talk with her, sit beside her, hold her, protect her.

It is not easy being sent here century after century. One soon learns to keep one's heart untouched. I felt nothing when I saw Lot's wife's face melt into a block of salt. I was simply doing my job.

Centuries of obedience. Centuries of doing my job well. Centuries of feeling little emotion about these pitiful creatures. Centuries of respecting the deep magic of the Master's plan. Then, suddenly, the moment my eyes drank in the sight of Diana, it felt like my heart was starving to consume this lovely woman's essence.

My assignment had nothing to do with Diana. I was sent to rescue a scrap of a Chinese baby girl struggling to survive. I saved the baby, of course, and quickly ushered the infant through to its adoption by the couple the Maker had chosen to raise it. Then, mission accomplished, instead of pulling my cloak of immortality around me and leaving this plane of existence, I went back to the orphanage, drawn there by not much more than a young woman's smile.

Diana was not strictly Chinese. Nor was she fully Caucasian. I, who had seen all the permutations of

DNA develop and change over the years could not place her at first. There was an air of exotic beauty about her that made me wonder if she might have been born on some distant island. As I examined her closer I saw that she had the markers of an extinct Bolivian tribe also flowing in her veins and a touch of Viking. An unusual mixture that had worked together well to have created this rare creature.

As I gazed into her spirit, I saw something disturbing. She had been an orphan in this place before an American family had adopted her, and I saw a middle-aged Chinese woman, sick and in pain, working over a vat of laundry not far from where I stood. I knew instantly that this was Diana's birth mother. I also knew that the woman was still heart-sick over having been forced to be parted from her only daughter.

It was at that moment I felt a great compassion come over me and I wanted to do something to help these two women. Without consulting the Maker, I decided that I would go ahead and take care of this situation on my own.

It was not my job to make a decision like that. I am not privy to the Maker's thoughts. I stupidly thought it would not hurt to bring them together. I suppose deep down, I wanted to make myself look important to the woman I loved and to her mother.

Before bringing them together, I spent the next two weeks reveling in the experience of getting to know her. We took long walks together. I showed her all the interesting places I knew in Beijing. Together we worked as volunteers in that orphanage. She had no idea that I was only temporarily in mortal form. I could feel her beginning to care for me, and that knowledge was sweet.

I continued to studiously avoid contact with the Maker.

I won't go into the details of how I brought them together, but I felt a great joy when I saw the mother's delight and relief over being reunited with her daughter. Diana's happiness was as great as I had hoped.

I thought I had done a wonderful thing. Diana and her mother agreed. I instantly became a hero in their eyes. Then evil slipped in.

An older, violent and half-crazed brother was not pleased over his mother's delight in finding her daughter. He grew extremely jealous and my beloved was gone within the week.

It was then that I suddenly found myself jerked back into my immortal form. The Maker had seen enough of me floundering around on my own among the mortals that he chose to bring me back for my own good. I am no longer given assignments that take me there.

As an immortal, I will never die. Many mortals would be envious of someone who would never have to taste death, but they would be wrong. To be immortal after losing someone like Diana means facing an eternity of emptiness and regret.

The Maker, seeing my pain, has recently given me a choice. I can, if I choose, go back into my mortal form on this planet. But if I do so choose, it will have to be a permanent thing. I will not be allowed to come back. I will be left to suffer and die alongside the other inhabitants of earth.

I did not know I would be given this choice. It is a great gift. I have made my decision gladly and easily. Immortality is not a gift when one is tortured with memories and mistakes. Tomorrow I am scheduled to embrace my mortality and I will be given a permanent body that will slowly wind down. I am fine with that.

In the meantime, I have another job to do. There is someone else I must find. The one who took Diana's precious life is hiding somewhere. The Maker will not tell me where he is, but I intend to seek him out.

In discovering the ability to love, I have also discovered the ability to hate.

I know my life's work now. It will be finding and destroying the man who took my beloved. I can hardly wait to receive my mortal form for the last time.

PURPLE DEFEATS THREE

DEREK E. MILLER

I traveled thousands of miles in Afghanistan. I would always see these nooks and caves while traveling the roads. Always wanted to go exploring and would think what if....

Dr. Shepherd sat in the forest green Toyota Hilux waiting for the all-clear to get out of the truck and walk up the steep embankment. Security Officer Dan Smite stood outside the truck door, ready to lift his gun at any moment.

"Sir, you should get the all-clear in a few minutes," Dan said. "We're just making sure there aren't any more hidden bombs or unexploded ordnances."

"That's fine," Dr. Shepherd said. "Whatever's there has been waiting on us for a thousand years."

"I just hope we kept the locals from stealing anything before we got here."

Dr. Shepherd nodded. "It would be a shame if anything was stolen.

"I just can't believe our luck," Dan said. "The drone strike not only took out one of the top leaders of the Taliban but also exposed the entrance. Thanks goodness our battle assessment observation saw that something wasn't right."

"It was a lucky break."

Dan's radio crackled to life. "All clear," the voice on the radio said. "Send the doctor up."

"Ok doc," Dan said. "Let's see if anything is in there that is actually worth all this."

Dr. Shepherd stepped out of the truck onto the dry brown Afghan soil. Long careful strides brought him to a gaping hole in the side of the mountain. Visible in the hole were parts of what had once been a doorway. There was explosive damage done that could never be replaced if, in fact, this was what he thought.

The huge stones that had been blown apart were

still in large chunks. What caught the eye of everyone there was the language that had been carved into those stones. It was unmistakably Greek.

Shepherd placed his hands on the stones.

"Hey doc, what do they say?" Dan asked.

"Can't say yet," Dr. Shepherd said, with studied nonchalance. "I need to brush off the dust and try to put a few words together. But who knows at this point?"

Shepherd clicked on his head lamp and stepped inside. He knew what the words said, but he did not want to give away his excitement. If this was what he thought it was he might be ridiculed at first, but then scholars would begin to recognize this as the discovery of a lifetime.

Deeper into the hole Shepherd went. He worried about the structural integrity of the obviously man-made cave. It looked well-built, but you never knew when explosives were involved. Especially uncontrolled explosives used to take out enemy forces.

By his best guess, after a few minutes, he was one hundred meters underground. All along the walls were the most beautiful carvings of Greek language and what looked to be supernatural scenes.

He came to a large wooden door. The dry air of Afghanistan had kept it from rotting. Other than being dusty, he was sure it looked just like it did when installed a thousand years ago.

Dr. Shepherd leaned against the door. The loud groan of hinges as they began to move after standing unmoved for centuries was deafening in the tight dark place.

Once the door was open Dr. Shepherd looked around with intensity. There was nothing where his flashlight shown except the stone floor in front of him. He kept moving forward. Could the locals already have cleaned out what was here? He stopped. There was undisturbed dirt on the floor, the sign that this find hadn't been touched yet.

After walking another twenty meters he found what he was looking for. In what he presumed was the dead center of the room was the most beautiful gold and marble pedestal. Sitting atop the pedestal was a ball of deep purple.

Dr. Shepherd fought his urge to reach out and grab it. There were carvings all over the pedestal in ancient Greek and he was not as familiar with it as he should be. He sat down and pulled an old Greek dictionary out of his backpack. Within it was a bookmark, a single playing card, the three of clubs.

Digging into his book, the Greek swirled in his

head and the loosely translated words slowly formed the words that his brain understood.

"Beware anyone who touches the Soul of Delilah."

Additional members from the research team that had followed Dr. Shepherd came into the room. He was irritated that another person invaded his space before he finished examining it.

"Goodness this is huge. Glad I brought a floodlight," Lisa said.

Wonderful Lisa, Dr. Shepherd's prize student and fellow researcher. At thirty-two Lisa had earned her stripes traveling the world with him to the most outlandishly dangerous places. Dr. Shepherd had questioned her hard when she first applied to his program years ago. Being the most sought-after researcher in obscure ancient cultures made him popular with the military at times like these. He had chosen his team very carefully. Lisa was one of the best

"Light it up," he said.

Lisa did as instructed. She aimed the flood light at the ceiling and when she flipped the switch the images that appeared on the ceiling and round walls were awe-inspiring.

The most gruesome yet beautiful pictures could be seen.

On the top was an image of a women holding a ball surrounded by thousands of soldiers lying dead on the ground. The purple waves that came out of it seemed to touch all the men in their chest.

"What is this place?" Lisa asked.

"I believe we found the real reason why Alexander the Great came to Afghanistan," he said.

"I know he came as part of his path to conquer the world but what is this?"

"There was a legend that there was a dangerous object with great power that he was searching for. It seems someone else found it before he arrived and challenged him for control of it. The object would give whoever held it power to control the world."

Lisa came closer to the pedestal.

"Back away Lisa. That's a dangerous object if even one percent of the legend is true."

"I'll be careful, professor."

Dr. Shepherd continued to study the pages of his ancient Greek translation book, but terror was forming in his heart as he continued to translate the words he saw written around the room.

He glanced up just as Lisa reached out.

"No!" he yelled, but he was too late.

The tip of Lisa's finger touched the ball. Her body went ridged and a blinding purple light came from the ball.

"What have you done?" Dr. Shepherd said, appalled.

Lisa did not speak.

Dr. Shepherd dropped his book and the bookmark fell out. He took a hard run at her, hoping to knock her free from the ball and break the connection.

He almost made it.

Within centimeters from reaching her, her right hand came up and it was like Dr. Shepherd had hit a wall. Blood poured from his split lip.

A deadly laugh came from Lisa's mouth, but it was not Lisa's laugh. Then ancient Greek flowed from her lips.

"Free. I am Free," she shouted. "Much too long sitting in darkness."

"Delilah?"

Lisa looked down at him on the ground. Her eyes were no longer Lisa's.

"Yes, I am Delilah. Your Ruler."

Dr. Shepherd slowly stood up. He knew he could be seeing the end of humanity unless he acted fast. Based on what he had translated he knew she would be weak at this point, and needed souls for more power.

"Delilah, how long have you been captive in here?"

"Time means nothing to me. One day or a million years, being trapped one moment is an eternity for me. Who are you?"

"Just a simple follower of yours."

"Good, good. I can feel the power coming from you."

Dr. Shepherd held something in his hand. He would only have one shot.

"I heard rumors but I did not know how beautiful you were until this moment."

A light laugh came from Lisa's mouth.

"Your compliments are well received, human."

"It is my honor to worship you and your beauty."

Dr. Shepherd moved slightly closer to her.

One shot, one shot is all he would have.

"If I had not eaten in so long I would keep you, but I must have your soul."

"I'm afraid I would not be very satisfying. My soul is dark," he said.

She started to reach out.

"But my soul is yours to have."

At that moment Dr. Shepherd threw the three of clubs into the air distracting her for just a moment.

It was all he needed. Lisa's eyes darted and he slammed himself into her as hard as he could to break the connection between her and the ball.

He felt a thousand punches to his gut. It was worse than being electrocuted. But he felt the crunch of them both hitting the ground. Lisa screamed as the connection was broken and the ball rolled away.

Lisa didn't breath for a long time but finally Dr. Shepherd felt her gasp for air.

"Doc, what happened?"

"Well, Lisa, we just about destroyed humanity as we know it. The soul of Delilah came through you."

"I'm so sorry I touched it."

"I should have been paying more attention," he said.

"What is this thing?"

"Alexander the Great was thought to come to Afghanistan in search of conquering the area. It was the furthest thing from the truth. He had heard of a great power in this area killing all of the men and women in its path. This evil, whatever it is, feeds on the souls of the living."

"How did he manage to capture it?"

"That part of the story is unknown. We know he

returned with very few men left after his journey here. He must have known what a danger it was and decided to bury it deep."

"Not deep enough."

No, but we must bury it deep now. This thing is too dangerous for anyone to touch or control.

Dr. Shepherd helped Lisa stand up and they started walking out.

"What is going to happen now?"

"I'm going to make sure no one can ever find this," he said.

They made their way out of the cave and met up with their security team.

"No one enters that hole," Dr. Shepherd said. "I want it filled with concrete as soon as possible. Fill it all up do you understand?"

"Yes sir," Dan said. "I'll see to it immediately."

Dr. Shepherd knew how dependable Dan was, and knew his instructions would be followed to the last detail.

"I believe we are going to be safe now," he said, as he turned to look at Lisa.

"Yes, I believe I am safe," she said. "But you are not."

Lisa's eyes had turned purple.

THE REPLACEMENT

JESSE R. LYLE

When I was younger, I enjoyed playing with fire (safely of course) and still to this day, fire fascinates me. How it moves and how its' patterns are seemingly random, but what if there was something working behind the scenes that was controlling the fire?

The smoke was heavy as Nikki drove to the scene of the house engulfed in flames. She was the first one there and quickly called in the fire to dispatch. She had just been driving through the sleepy village and wasn't ready for this. It had only been a week since her orientation onto the force and she was still wet behind the ears, but she wasn't going to let that stop her.

As she got out of her mini pumper truck and approached, she felt the thick wave of heat hit her as the front windows cracked, letting in a gust of oxygen, fueling the already ruthless fire.

"Unit 23. Come in Nikki. Over," a voice crackled over the radio.

"Unit 23 here. Over," Nikki responded while the flames licked around the gutters and danced on the roof.

"We've got another unit in route to your location," the voice said.

Good. How the heck could I have handled this mess myself?

"Sam and Michael are on their way. Over," the voice spat in her ear one more time.

Even better. She wouldn't mind help from anyone, but with Sam she knew everything would be okay.

The temperature around the house was becoming very uncomfortable and she started stepping back. As far as she knew the house had been abandoned for several years now and didn't show any signs of someone living there. She wasn't sure how the fire had started, maybe a lightning strike or teenagers playing a prank that got out of hand.

There wasn't much she could do with her truck, it had a 250 gallon tank and enough water to provide her with about five minutes of coverage. Its only usefulness now would be to help keep the fire from spreading to other things like the storage building nearby.

She heard the familiar siren off in the distance letting her know she wouldn't be alone for much longer. Seconds passed, feeling like an eternity, waiting for Sam and Michael to get there. The sound of her comrades coming as fast as they could should have been a comfort to her, but there was something different about this fire.

She'd seen plenty of videos and experienced several training simulations. She *knew* which route a fire would take. She *knew* how much time certain materials needed before spontaneously combusting from the heat. She *knew* that there wasn't much she, or her backup, would be able to do but keep it from spreading and let the house inevitably burn down.

It felt strange to witness this particular fire, with its unique pattern of travel and how it appeared to ignore certain areas of the house. It appeared to engulf the entire house, except for one area at the front where the door used to be. *The fire should be searching for oxygen through the front opening. There's nothing there to keep it from coming out… there's no door, probably torn off by some neighborhood kids. Nothing there but blackness.* At that moment her mouth went dry. She saw something she had been training for, but secretly wished she would never see—the silhouette of a person in the window of the second floor.

Having finished putting her gear on, she did the opposite of what everyone would and should do. She started running towards the fire.

"Nikki! What are you doing?!" Sam shouted over the radio as he and Michael pulled their rig into the overgrown driveway.

She didn't have time to explain, but managed to get out a few words into her portable radio in between her breaths as she ran straight through the front door opening. "Person. Second floor. East window."

The house was constructed similarly to some of the other old homes in the area. With its basic square layout, it had a couple of large rooms on the main floor, a straight stairwell on the west side, and several bedrooms upstairs.

As she rushed in wearing only her basic gear and respirator, she noticed a void in the fire and smoke, almost like a channel of water with a current rushing below the surface. All the smoke and fire swirled around the void but where she stood was calm and clear.

The tunnel through the fire twisted and turned toward the stairwell and she took the opportunity to sprint in the direction of the stairs. Expecting to see the banister eaten away by fire, it surprised her to see the stairs and banister fully intact as if they hadn't been touched by the immense heat all around them.

With just a moment's hesitation she ran up the stairs silently giving thanks they were still strong enough to carry her.

"Nikki! We've got a hose trained on the east side. What's your twenty? We don't want to block your path with our water!" a voice asked across the radio.

"I just reached the second floor. West side. Keep that hose in place. I'm sweeping through to the east."

"Copy that." Sam said, as he gave the thumbs up to Michael who had planted himself ready for the heavy stream of water to gush out of the hose he was holding.

Nikki didn't know what was going on, but the corridor upstairs had that same void of smoke and fire leading to the east side of the house. She stopped only for a moment at each doorway along the hallway as she made her way to the last room. The first six doorways were either missing their door or were open and raging in fire.

She hastened her search to the last room, where the door was closed and had light shining through the seven frosted glass spade cutouts arranged evenly on the door. She reached to grab the doorknob, frantic but determined. Since she had risked her life this far into the house, she might as well confirm whether a person needed saving.

Her hand touched the knob, and she quickly recoiled. She expected it to be hot to the touch, but what frightened her was how cold the doorknob was. This difference in temperature made the knob feel like it was burning her with heat, yet it was cold even through the gloves she wore. She reached a second time, resolved to open this barricade before her.

The door opened easily, with no resistance as if the door was being pulled opened from the other side. As the door swung open she heard something through the deafening sound of the house burning and crashing down around her. A sound she couldn't place. A sound that shouldn't be there. A sound that cut right through, deep to her bones.

She then felt the pull. It came from the center of the room, a room not charred by the fire, not touched by the smoke, and not doused by the water. The pull was strong and caught her off guard. Without warning she realized she wasn't being pulled so much as being pushed by some force traveling through the empty void she'd just come through earlier in the house.

The void was rapidly closing. Pushing all of its air and pressure towards her to force her into this room. She turned around and saw a wall of light, hungry for the oxygen held within the void. The fire was climbing the stairs and turning the corner. Faster and faster it sped through the hallway coming right for her. She slammed the door.

She could feel the heat on the other side of the door and knew she only had a few moments before the whole house would collapse. She turned and saw that the room was well lit, but she was not sure of the source. She decided it must be the reflections of the fire. The room was mostly bare except for the person standing by the window. She lunged toward the person, who must be saved.

When Nikki opened her eyes she felt at ease and peaceful. As time passed she soon began to panic as she discovered she was unable to move any of her limbs. She was propped up in front of the window just close enough to see through it. Outside she could spot her fellow firefighters expertly controlling the steady stream of water that gushed against the roof right outside her window.

"Thank you." a voice whispered.

"Help!" Nikki choked out.

"Thank you." The voice repeated.

"I can't move!" Nikki coughed, succumbing to the smoke starting to fill the room.

"Thank you." She heard the voice say again.

"For what?" Nikki cried out.

"For being the seventh," the voice said with finality.

"The seventh what?" Nikki languished.

From her vantage point, Nikki could just barely see the scene outside, but saw a figure approaching Sam and Michael. Something was oddly familiar about the figure. She saw it gesture with its arm in a direction away from the house. The water stopped drenching the area near the window and moved to the trees nearby. The lack of water hitting the roof and splashing onto the window finally gave Nikki a clear view.

With Sam and Michael focused on keeping the surroundings from catching fire, the figure turned towards Nikki and trained its focus on her. As it stared at her, Nikki could hear something whispering in her head. "Thank you for being the seventh sacrifice, and setting me free."

As the figure pulled its respirator off, Nikki saw a look of satisfaction and accomplishment on its face, and wondered why that face belonged to her.

HILT

A. B. ALVAREZ

The reaction humans have to stress is always a thing to behold. What would you do if you were surrounded by a life you didn't create, but nonetheless had to take responsibility for? What would you do if a ghost just wouldn't leave you alone?

I felt the heavy knife tug at the waistband of my dress and wondered if it would get the sort of use I expected of it.

When my husband died, quite unexpectedly, my mind was unable to comprehend the seriousness of what had transpired. Here on the southern tip of England in what was ostensibly his family's castle, I lived at the beck and call of my spouse apart from my family and friends, apart from the life I lived so many years ago, apart from the person I knew so well. Life here had its own rhythm and my husband, Garth, had made it his own.

Many times I wished for relief from his intensity. The waves pounding against the nearby cliffs were a constant reminder of the uncontrollable even as I sought some measure of stability. Childless, friendless, and without nearby neighbors the time spun downward in slowly tightening spirals affording me no relief.

Upon the death of Garth, the worst began: bill collectors began coming to our home (*our* because I still think of Garth as being with me, an apparition of unholy solidity) as more and more of our financial life, which I took for granted, was revealed to be a sham.

And there were his visits in the middle of the night.

But this was the evening I had both feared and longed for. After many days and nights of loneliness and terror (after all, how can one not be afraid of visitations from the dead while sleeping?) I had called for a séance asking the local constable to arrange to have a Mrs. Willoughby, who was well known in these parts, come and help me talk to my recently deceased husband.

When the first knock came, I knew it would be one of Garth's closest associates. A man, a brute, if truth be told, by the name of Henry Ascot who had come to my home often with the excuse of performing chores Garth had required of him on a regular basis. He and my handmaiden took care of the overall tending of our large and foreboding residence since my move from the north after my arranged marriage.

I opened the door and let in Henry Ascot. As per his usual appearance, his clothes were filthy from the nooks and crannies where he worked. His thick mustache held flecks of dust and paint and his jacket, an unusual shade of chimney brown, was covered in black freckles. His face was otherwise unshaven. I, in my heavy black dress, whose skirt ran from my waist down to my feet, felt protected by the thick cloth covering me from neck to ankles. My hair, tied in the tidy bun I prefer when home, sat perfectly in position toward the rear of my head.

Over the time of my marriage, the castle in all of its regal splendor had become more the symbol of Garth's shadow over my life and less a safe haven where a roaring fire could warm my body as well as my soul. No, the problems that have beset me after his death, if death it was, were always there in the background, hiding like a squirrel who did not want to be seen, or a storm cloud whose sudden appearance changed the timbre of the day and who's lightning somehow missed the guilty but set the innocent ablaze.

Ascot knew his way around so I let him go before me down to the lower chambers of the stone and candlelit area. I rarely went down into the damp bowels of the castle for fear of losing my way, similar to how my way had been lost so many years ago.

I felt the scraping sound of the door knocker before I heard the three blows against the door. I ran back up in the gray light hoping for Mrs. Willoughby, as no one else was expected this evening. The assorted lot of men with their arms outstretched looking for money, or crops, or worse, would continue to arrive until the castle was disposed of and the monies given to all those to whom Garth had made promises the living had to keep.

Mrs. Willoughby stood before me as I swung the thick wooden door open. She was as I remembered: dark features beneath pale skin. Sunken eyes that might as well have been all black with a head of curly dark hair framing her almond shaped face. She wore white lace over her face, but her dirty beige top, and dark brown skirt flowed to her feet which were encased in the work boots I would expect to see on a man. She nodded.

"Good evening, Mrs. Brody," she said. Her voice was soft, almost a whisper. This was the woman who could speak into the great beyond and get me the answer I sought. Her birdlike hand reached up and I held it in both of mine. The cold of the countryside channel itself though her body into my hands. Would tonight turn out as I required? As I so sorely needed?

"Did he visit you again last night?" she asked. Her eyes, open wide and yet just barely opened, peered into mine and I knew I could not lie.

"He did. He came again when I thought myself slumbering, fearfully half-awake yet half-asleep." I remembered last night. He did not appear every evening, but often enough to question my sanity. Was it simply a dream? Would I not shed the anguish his visage created deep in my heart and in my soul?

"Fear not," Mrs. Willoughby said, squeezing my left hand. Tonight, you will see that he is here for you and will never leave you in isolation or in anything less than peace.

Fear? Isolation? If I could find isolation perhaps I could find a measure of peace.

I led her down to the cellar, the stone wall sweating from the humidity of the dense sea air. I lightly touched it and felt the slight greasy texture of the wet stones. The boulders that held my home together. The formation I could not wait to leave.

The plain wooden table, illuminated by a collection of candles, lay within a circle of light surrounded by a darkness that hid my misgivings.

The visions of last night haunted me. Garth came to me. He took me and I had no strength to resist. Helpless to stop him, I was powerless to awaken. The nightmares of my waking moments, once thought past, were now part of the night where sleep was as unstoppable as his desire for me from the grave.

Aston sat at one end of the square brown table. He had brought it down a few days earlier when I first broached the possibility of contacting Garth. His reaction was to be expected. He laughed and told me to accept my fate; God had chosen a path for me and his spirits would do what they would. If Garth was coming to me then it was the will of a higher power.

My heart sank at his words. Tonight I would determine their truth. Tonight, I would test if this was the work of God or Satan.

Mrs. Willoughby sat to my left and Aston to my right. The flat sounds of the chairs gently pulled across the floor was all I heard as we took our positions. The medium pulled back the lace from her face and I could see her porcelain visage. Except for the hardness of her eyes her face held all the vibrancy of youth. She was beautiful.

She lay out a selection of tarot cards in a familiar pattern. The ones that leapt into my attention were The Fool, and the Four of Cups. The latter hung upside down from a tree. The former filled with dark red blood.

Garth had admitted to visiting her for divine advice. Aston confirmed his stories. They would often go to see her alone, but I knew that many times Aston returned without Garth. Perhaps Garth sought other types of advice.

Mrs. Willoughby reached out for my hand and I to Aston. Her cool smooth hands fell lightly in my grip while Aston's were course, like roughly ground sandpaper. My stomach turned at his touch.

We closed our eyes. Mrs. Willoughby intoned the sighs and hums of her spells into the ether as my back felt a chill. I looked up. I thought I saw a shadow. The darkness engulfed my vision, my sight, and my emotions. The whites of my eyes lost their ability to see as the darkness encroached on my perception of time and place.

Garth stepped into the light. He wore a heavy cloth cap that cast a shadow across his face down to his chest forming a point in the middle of his shirt. He wore the last clothes I had seen him in: a white shirt with a telltale tear approximately half way down his arm. Dark trousers making his legs look a part of the surrounding black, and shoes stained with mud. His shoes were always stained in mud.

"Garth," I said.

He stood unmoving.

"Why?"

Mrs. Willoughby spoke in a flat tone. The voice she possessed when possessed. "He cannot leave this plane. His destiny is with you and this home he made with you."

I released their hands. Neither moved, their hands suspending where I left them. Perhaps they lowered them perhaps not. I walked over to my dead husband.

He turned toward me, his sallow face still covered by the shadow of his cap.

"Why?"

Still he said nothing. His right hand reached and grabbed my left as terror gripped my soul. He pulled me closer. I could smell his sweat and the sea and the mud. The grass. The mildew.

His face approached mine. My shoulders tensed.

This was a new version of what had happened to me every night. Every night when he would come to me and take me and leave me hurt and spent and vengeful.

With my right hand, unseen by the others, I reached into the pocket of my skirt. The deep pocket.

His face engulfed mine. His lips pressed themselves against me. I could taste the whiskey and the stale breath from his lungs.

I pulled back enough to allow entry of my right hand between us as I plunged the knife I had pulled from my dress pocket as deep and as hard as I could under and up into his chest and turned the hilt. He gasped. He reached out to me. I stepped back.

The sleeping draughts that his servants, still loyal to him, had been giving me had made me compliant during his visits, but his death before his mistress and best friend was final. Garth fell with a flat sound in the otherwise empty chamber. His blood poured out of the wound below his ribcage where the knife had made a puncture large enough for him to bleed his life on the dirty cold floor and I could finally sleep in peace.

DEATH BY FOUR

DEREK E. MILLER

While in Afghanistan, I was indirectly responsible for an American Girl and a Swedish guy meeting and falling in love. They decided to get married in Las Vegas and I had the privilege of being invited to the wedding. It was my first time to Vegas. I'm not a gambler and horrible card player but I'm a good people watcher. I found watching gambling much more interesting. I saw lives destroyed and fortunes made, what if…

Ruth sat on the grey concrete porch steps. Her white sundress lay limp on her legs on this warm windless night. It was getting darker and darker. The street lights had come on a short time ago. Her soul filled with dread. It was payday and her husband was not home.

He promised… He promised he was done, but she knew in her heart he was not.

Ruth's knee bounced up and down with each passing of the second hand on the inexpensive silver Timex watch around her wrist.

She shifted her body wondering how she would pay the rent this month, how to pay for food, how to pay the electric bill. The weekly paycheck was, no doubt, already gone into the pit of snakes.

Why Jerry could not stop his gambling she never knew. Over and over again he had promised her "last night with the boys was the last time."

A year ago he had been beat up so badly he was in the hospital for two weeks. They still owed the hospital on that medical bill. He owed too much money to the local mafia who ran the illegal back room poker games. They would never be able to pay it back. She was grateful they didn't come after her or their infant son, Frankie, to send a message.

She thought that being beat up so badly would have taught him the lesson he needed to learn to provide for his family and not fuel his gambling high.

When the headlights came around the corner she knew. She just knew what was going to happen.

The long black Cadillac slowly came down the street and came to a stop in front of her house. Two huge men got out of the back seat, opened the trunk, pulled out a huge heap and dumped it in the front yard.

She didn't move until the car had driven away. Then she rushed over. Kneeling, she slowly turned the large heap over. Groaning in pain, her husband looked up at her.

"Honey I'm so sorry." Jerry said

She looked down with love, pity, and hatred.

"You destroyed our family," Ruth said. "I love you, but you are a stupid, stupid man."

She immediately felt remorse that those were the last words he heard as he took his last breath.

Then she started to weep. As the tears ran down her cheeks, it was bizarre, she actually felt relief. She wouldn't have to worry anymore about what would happen once the musical chairs stopped and the gambling caught up to her family. It was here, and Ruth and her baby son were still alive.

Ruth reached over and closed her husband's eyes. She placed her hands on his hands and felt something in them. She took hold of the object and held it up to her face. It was the Four of Spades.

"Dad, its easy money in the dorms."

"Son, Nothing easy about gambling. House always win and I mean always."

"Dad, it's just poker for fun and I'm cleaning up."

"I don't care, your grandfather made my mother and me homeless fifty year ago with just-for-fun poker and it took years to rebuild our lives. She never completely healed. It drove her mad and into an early grave."

"We just play for fun money."

"Your grandmother swore on her death bed she would come back and haunt anyone in our family that ever gambled."

"Whatever, Dad. It's different times."

"I swear I believed her. You have no idea how bad my dad hurt us. No home, no food, no hope. Something like that burns within someone's spirit even after they're long gone. Whenever your grandmother saw a deck of cards she would start shaking."

"My hands don't shake."

"Son please, put the cards away. You can't win. Promise me."

"Sure dad I promise."

Justin couldn't sleep. The nightmares kept coming. Him in Vegas hanging on by a thread. His grandmother screaming at him to stop. But he couldn't just stop. The thrill was too great. Even cocaine was not as addictive as winning a huge pot. Poker was the love of his life. Tomorrow would be do or die.

But Justin also knew there was a chance that things could go south and he would never be heard from again. He had a strong desire to call his dad.

"Hey son, what's up?"

"Dad tell me again about the night grandpa died."

"Well that's a way to open a conversation. Mom wouldn't hardly talk about it. All I know from what my mom told me was that he was in too deep to the mob. He went out gambling and lost so much they knew he could never pay it back. They beat him so badly that he died. They just threw his body out in his yard. In his hand was a four of spades. It was like their sign to her and others in the neighborhood don't gamble what you can't pay back."

The phone was silent for a long time.

"Dad, I'm in trouble. I'm in deep like grandpa."

"Oh son, where are you? I'll hide you."

"It's too late dad, today is do or die.

"It's never too late, son."

"I'm such a disappointment. Grandma keeps haunting me in my dreams."

"I promise it's not too late, Where are you?"

"Dad, I swear I'll win. I love you."

The phone went silent. Justin's dad silently wept.

Justin sat there at the table. He was all in. He couldn't lose. He worked so hard on making sure he didn't give any tells. The pile of cash in front of him was huge. He had enough to pay off his loan shark and still be way ahead. So far ahead he could pay his father back.

He could have walked away and been in the clear, but just one more hand. Just one more hand.

His grandmother's face kept entering his mind. He felt like he was going crazy. He swore he was hearing her speak to him. It was like she was in the room standing behind him. Warning him if he didn't stop he would never have a family. She would see to it he could not destroy someone else's life.

The heavy Russian accent took him out of his trance.

"You must be very confident in your hand, no?"

Justin did not react. He could not give out his tell. Did not want to give away his hand. Staring back at him he had one ace and one king. On the table was an Ace of Diamonds, an Ace of Clubs, a four of hearts. The odds of him being beat by anything else was so remote it was worth taking the chance of being all in and ending this game.

"I have random cards like everyone else. You going to play?"

The Russian laughed and slowly pushed the rest of his money in.

"You know most of that pile already belongs to me even if you win."

"Yes, but I'll be free of my debt to you."

"But if you lose you won't see tomorrow and I get all your cash."

The fourth card was dealt out. It was a Jack of Diamonds.

Justin knew he had this won. He would be free of his debt. The ghost of his grandmother would be banished forever. She would be out of his dreams and he would not feel like she was staring over his shoulder the whole time.

"Are you ready for the river? It's do or die for you my little friend."

Justin kept his face straight. No bouncing of his legs. His hands were steady.

"Deal it."

The absolute celebration he felt in his heart could not be constrained. There the last card was turned. It was a junk card. He had won with his three aces.

"I won! You can suck it Victor. I'm free."

Justin stood, ready to do a victory dance. He had a full house!

The Russian was silent. But then the most evil of grins cross his face.

"Oh, you stupid kid."

Two of Victor's muscle men started to come up behind him. Suddenly the hair on the back of Justin's neck stood upright. Something was wrong. Then he realized Victor had not shown his cards. Justin was sick to his stomach.

He felt the hands come up and grab his shoulders. He turned to Victor as he flipped over his cards. Two fours. It took another second for Justin to process. With the fourth and final four showing, Victor had won, beating Justin with his three aces. A four of kind beat a full house.

Justin's head processed his fate as he was lifted up by the two huge thugs. He heard a cackle in his ears and knew it was his grandmother. The river card that had been flipped over was the worst possible card. What were the odds? The same card that had killed his grandfather was looking back up from the table. There before him was the last card he would ever see. The Four of Spades.

THE CALLING CARD

SERENA B. MILLER

Forgiving oneself can be difficult, especially for an Amish mother.

I have never known what to do with anger. After all, Amish women are not supposed to experience any. We are taught to be a forgiving people, content with our lives, serene and faithful no matter what the circumstances.

I know what I am supposed to do. The problem is doing it. Especially when anger pitches and boils inside of me until I think I must explode or lose my mind.

I am not angry at the bishop of our church, nor

am I angry at the church members. I am not angry at any of my relatives, although some of them do get on my nerves. I am not angry at my husband, Obediah. At least not *very* angry. Maybe I'm a little bit angry at him.

Sometimes I get a little angry at the tourists, the "Amish *lieben*" who come into my small shop. "Amish *lieben*" is a derisive term. It means "Amish lovers." We privately use it to make fun of outsiders who revere all things Amish. Like the people who exclaim over the handmade items we have for sale, and think our children are too cute for words.

These Amish *lieben* people have no concept of the back-breaking labor that goes into the creating of our lifestyle they admire so much, or the sacrifices. For instance, gardening is considered women's work in our culture. Outsiders cannot know how difficult it is to bend over to weed and harvest while so often pregnant.

Some of these tourists are even foolish enough to fantasize aloud about how they wish they could be part of our community. They don't know what they are talking about. One has to be born and raised in this culture to endure it.

That is not a complaint. It is a fact. There is a level of work that takes a toll on all of us, but especially the women. Sometimes it takes a very great toll. We often feel unwell, but because we are Amish and much is expected of us, we often work in spite of our illnesses.

I am a dutiful wife who respects her husband as is commanded. I honor him with my actions and my words. I accept his leadership in our home. He is a fair man, frequently kind, when he can remember to be so, and has never physically hurt me or my children. I have no idea if I love him anymore, but that does not matter.

Obediah does expect a standard of competence that has been hard for me to achieve. Especially considering the fact that our children came quickly, one after another, in quick succession. Keeping eight children dressed and fed is not easy. It would have been nice had he hired some help for me, but he did not see the need.

Perhaps if he had, we would not have lost Phillip. That is why I struggle with anger against him.

I suppose compared to most *Englisch* women I would be considered a good mother and wife, but compared to my Amish sisters, I am frequently judged as lacking in domestic ability.

"My ten-year-old daughter is a better quilter than you, Gretchen, "my sister, Hilda, once said. We were having a quilting frolic and I was failing at making the tiny stitches required. I flushed at her criticism and tried harder.

The truth of the matter is that of all the chores that fall to me, I hate sewing the most. I despise everything about it. Not only am I not good at it, I always get a headache and my back will ache for days after making an article of clothing. Unfortunately, our particular sect of conservative Amish requires that we wear handmade clothing only.

As the number of children in my household increased, keeping my family clothed involved an enormous amount of sewing. I lived my life dreading the drudgery of it.

My son, Phillip, was growing like a weed. He was fourteen and I could barely keep him fed, let alone clothed. It seemed like I would sew one pair of pants in the evening and by the end of the next day he would have grown another three inches and his ankles would be showing again.

The day before the tragedy, I had not been feeling well. I was nauseous and tired and newly pregnant with our ninth child. Sitting at my treadle sewing machine, making yet another pair of boys' pants was the last thing I felt like doing. I should have asked one of my sisters to help me, but I am a prideful woman.

I did not want to let them know that I could not keep up. I did not want them making fun of me.

There was to be a picnic at my husband's brother's farm. We Amish spend a great deal of time together. All the family was going. I would rather have stayed home and rested, but my sister-in-law is prickly, and I knew she would be upset if I begged off.

My son, Phillip, did not have pair of pants that were long enough to wear to the picnic. He would have gone anyway and made a joke of it, but I was embarrassed. I made him stay home while the rest of us went. I promised to make him a new pair when I got back.

Lives can be destroyed by such small things.

I love all my children, but if a mother could admit to having a favorite son, for me it was Phillip. He was my oldest, the one who had been with me the longest, and he understood me in ways that the other children did not. It was Phillip who would notice when I was tired and help share my load of domestic chores without being asked. It was Phillip who would notice when I was especially tired, and bring me a cup of tea and tell me to rest while he watched the little ones.

It was a terrible thing that I had allowed such a

thoughtful son to go too long without a new pair of pants.

So Phillip stayed home and the rest of us left. He did not like being alone, so he walked up the road to visit one of his friends. It was an innocent thing. He did nothing wrong or forbidden.

I don't know why he did not hear the truck that killed him. Perhaps it swerved too quickly for him to jump out of the way. All I know is that a police car showed up at the picnic with the news that my Phillip was gone.

I lost two children that day. My beloved Phillip, and the babe that I was carrying beneath my heart.

We Amish do not wait long to bury a relative. Others did what was necessary. I was not able to participate. I remember nothing except falling into an emotional abyss.

They say that I huddled in Phillip's bed after the miscarriage. I clung to the pillow that still smelled of him, not allowing anyone to take it from me. Nor would I allow anyone to lead me to my own bed, the one I had shared with my husband. They say I screamed and fought anyone who tried to pull me from Phillip's room.

The young man who had been texting on his cell

phone, the one who swerved at the last minute and took my son's life, came to apologize.

From the cradle, we are taught to be a forgiving people, but I clawed at him. I wanted to hurt him. My husband held me back while others quickly ushered the young man out the door. My mind went blank again after that. I did not care if I ate or drank or took the pins out of my hair at night. I did not care if my children were fed or clothed. My mind, overwhelmed with pain, shut down.

It was probably a good thing. Had it not shut down, my own self-loathing would have been too great to allow me to continue to live. I blamed myself for Phillip's death.

It is hard to breathe when one is swimming in a lake of self-hatred. Let alone care for one's family. My husband, struggling with his own grief, was unable to focus on caring for our children. In the way of the Amish community my family was broken up and my children were temporarily parceled out to other members of our church.

Everyone felt sorry for these poor children who had lost a brother, an unborn baby sister, and had a crazy mother wandering the woods and fields like a lost soul. I lost my head covering somewhere along the way, and I allowed my waist-long hair to become tangled and wild. Soon, my clothes were torn to shreds from brambles and branches. I became filthy and I did not care.

My husband did not know what to do with me. I found myself rather gleeful over that fact. It felt strangely freeing to become an embarrassment to my church and my family…and to myself.

Some bereaved mothers haunt their child's grave, rearranging pebbles, clipping grass, their need to nurture still so strong within them that they are compelled to groom the very earth above their child's body.

I did not groom Phillip's grave, but I slept on top of it most nights—what little sleep I got. I also haunted the road where he had been killed. I was unkempt, wild-eyed, wild-haired, looking for any sign that Phillip had been there. It rained the terrible night after his death. A hard rain that poured into the gullies around our home, making rivulets where there had been none, and making creeks out of the rivulets, and then rivers where there was usually only streams. All traces of my child's blood was washed away, absorbed into the silent earth.

The bend where he died became a magnet to me. It is a wonder that I, too, did not lose my life spending so much time there. Local people learned to slow down before they came to that curve in the road, knowing that they would probably see a crazy Amish woman sitting there, plucking at the grass like a raccoon with distemper.

One day I saw what looked like a small piece of paper sticking out of the ground. It was a sodden playing card, black and white, a six of clubs. Phillip had confessed to me only two weeks earlier that he had learned to play a game called poker with some of his friends. They had bet with pebbles instead of money, and even though our church forbids the playing of poker, I did not see that there was anything so bad in what he had done. I did not discipline him for such a small infraction. Nor did I tell Obediah, who, as a deacon in our church, might have felt it necessary to punish him. To my way of thinking, playing a card game with pebbles was not so terrible.

Now, I gathered the little playing card to my heart, certain that it had somehow fallen out of my son's pocket. I looked to see if there were more cards, but there were not. I decided to take it home and put it in my son's room for safe keeping.

My husband was happy to see me come home that night. I had begun sleeping wherever I fell down. In barns, beneath trees. Waking up with the morning dew on my face and dress.

That night, he would not allow me to leave the house again. He physically restrained me from going. He told me that I could sleep in our son's bed for as long as I wanted if only I would stay inside our house for the night. He said he was ashamed of the fact that one of our neighbors had been frightened by me rising up from behind some bales of hay in his barn earlier that morning. He said he was going to stay up all night to make certain I did not leave. He took up a vigil outside my door.

I carefully put the precious playing card away in the top of Phillip's bureau, beneath his woolen socks, and lay down upon his bed.

Our beds are not soft like *Englisch* beds. They are thin and hard. In our particular sect, we do not allow ourselves much comfort. Sometimes I think that my people believe the more miserable we are here on earth the more likely it is that we will get to heaven.

My body was exhausted, my mind and heart were too, but I could not sleep. I lay upon the bed in my dirty clothes, my head resting on a pillow that still held a whiff of my son's scent and I stared at the ceiling. I was desperate to leave. The longer I stayed inside this house, the more I felt like I was suffocating. My hope was that my husband would soon relax his vigilance, fall asleep, and I could make my escape.

I lay there, hopeless, angry, and bereft of my other children who had been taken from me by the church. I did not blame the people for having done so, it was simply part of the endless cycle of pain that had become my life.

My son, Adam, had shared this room with Phillip. I looked at his bed and wondered if he would ever sleep in it again. He was staying with a family where the mother was everything I was not-a woman who cheerfully kept her family well-fed and well-clothed and made it look easy. It occurred to me that Adam probably preferred living there with her than at home with the crazy woman I had become. I wondered if my other children felt the same way. I thought about the babe I had lost and comforted myself with the knowledge that at least that little one had never experienced my failure as a mother.

Then it happened. The thing that saved my sanity and most probably my life.

I swear to you, with every drop of honesty that is in my heart, I was not asleep. I was hyper-awake when Phillip appeared at the foot of the bed, and he was smiling at me.

How do I describe it? Why even bother? No matter what I say, people will only believe that it was only another extension of my craziness.

But I know what I saw. It was Phillip standing there exactly as he was the day we left for the picnic. Strong and sturdy, his complexion ruddy from working outside, his eyes alight with fun and joy.

He was so real that I jumped out of bed thinking to embrace him. My broken mind believing his death had been nothing more than a terrible dream.

"Phillip!" I cried, my arms outstretched. "You've come back to me."

The compassion and love that I saw in his eyes were all Phillip's, but he held out his hand as though to stop me from coming closer.

"You must stop grieving, *Maam*," he said. "I am fine. It was not your fault. Now, go gather my little brothers and sisters. They miss you so."

He stopped speaking then, but stood looking at me with such great love and understanding that my breath caught in my throat and I forgot to breathe. Then he faded away.

When he was gone, I gasped for air, but I continued to stare at the spot where he had stood, wishing I could call him back. There was so much I wanted to say.

And then the other gift came. The strange warming of my heart that was so healing I found myself crossing my arms over my chest to hold the warm glow in as long as possible. The only way I can describe it is as an otherworldly glow. A peace entered my heart and slowly spread out, permeating every cell of my body.

I climbed back into bed after that, and tears began to leak from the corners of both eyes. They were no longer tears of grief, but healing tears, as the toxic pain I had been carrying drained from my soul. They quietly soaked my hair and the pillow.

My husband tells me that I slept eighteen hours straight. When I awoke, it was to a different world. I rose from the bed and began to tend to myself.

It took some time. My hair had become so matted and tangled I could not get a comb through it so I gave up and cut it all off at my shoulders with my sewing shears. Then I bathed and put on a dark lavender dress. My hair is curly and with it shorter, it felt soft and fluffy around my face. When I was finished, I almost looked like an *Englisch* woman.

My husband, who had gone to work while I continued to sleep, came home and found me dressed and in my right mind. He asked what had brought about this change and I told him I had seen Phillip.

My husband often says the wrong thing at the wrong time. Today was no exception. He told me that what I had seen was not possible. He said that ghosts do not exist. He forbade me from speaking about it to others. He told me to pin my short hair up under my prayer *kapp* and not let anyone know that I had cut it off.

I did not care much for my husband that day.

Instead of arguing, I went to Phillip's room and gathered up the tangled hair that was still lying on the floor, along with the torn and stained clothing I had shed. Obediah's words echoed in my ears and made me begin to doubt the reality of what I had seen. Had Phillip truly appeared to me? Had he really spoken those words of forgiveness and encouragement?

As I was sweeping up the last piece of hair, I saw the corner of something white lying beneath the braided rug where Phillip had stood. I pulled it out and gasped. It was a single playing card, identical to the one I had found on the side of the road where Phillip had breathed his last.

I ran to the bureau and opened the top drawer wondering if I was mistaken that I had placed the card beneath Phillip's socks. I was not mistaken. There it was. I held two identical playing cards in my hands. The coincidence was too great.

I will go to my grave believing that this was

Phillip's way of reassuring me that what I had seen was real.

I obeyed my husband. I did not speak to anyone about the visitation I had received from my son. I never again told anyone about those few moments of being drenched in Phillip's forgiveness and love.

My church breathed a collective sigh of relief, brought my children back to me one by one, and life went on the same as before. Except that nothing was ever the same as before.

I am committing all of this to paper while it is still fairly fresh in my mind, to remind myself of the validity of what I saw. In a bottom drawer in the bedroom I now once again share with my husband, I have hidden the two identical playing cards. When my husband is not at home and the children are all occupied, I sometimes take the cards out and look at them like an Englisch woman might look at photographs of her child. I look at these two cards and say, "Phillip *did* come back to me."

There will come a day when I might choose a different life. I no longer believe in the rules and regulations of our church. But for now I wash and clean and sew and help Obediah raise our children to adulthood. Once the children are raised and gone… well, I shall see.

ANCIENT RUNES

JESSE R. LYLE

I personally don't have any tattoos and I rarely get a chance to find out the meaning behind other people's ink. But what if knowing the meaning behind the ink, may not be a story you want to hear...

As the little boy looked up from his make shift meal of table scraps pulled from the dumpster behind the local Italian joint, he noticed something peculiar about the large man approaching him. He couldn't see the man's face, and only knew it was a man by the broad shoulders outlined by the flickering street lights behind the figure.

Jeffrey wasn't timid and he knew he might have to

fight for this little bit of sustenance he'd managed to scrape together.

"This is mine!" Jeffrey shouted.

The large man, built like a solid block chimney, towered so high he cast a shadow down on Jeffrey. The little boy stood and put his hands up, clenched into dirty, calloused fists of rage, ready to defend his spoils. Jeffrey knew he wouldn't win if the man really wanted his scraps, but he wasn't going down without a fight. He knew that if he gave up every time someone challenged him, he'd soon be nothing, and would probably be left to die, alone.

The man stopped just out of reach of Jeffrey's fists and kept his hands in the pockets of his trench coat.

With his eyes now starting to adjust to the darkness the large man threw in his direction, Jeffrey could tell this was someone who'd grown up with a hard life too. There was a scar across the man's face, and a scowl of contempt. Jeffrey knew he was done for.

Jeffrey relaxed his posture and dropped his fists. He changed tactics and squatted behind his unusual plate of scraps. Gesturing toward the man, he said, "I guess I've got some extra I can share with you if you're hungry."

The large man grunted, and collapsed his body so that he was sitting cross legged with the plate of abandoned food positioned between them. Jeffrey grabbed a half-eaten stick of garlic bread and tore it in two, handing the large man the slightly smaller half. The man took the stale bread and struggled with chewing a bite from it.

"Thanks," the man said under his breath.

"You're welcome," Jeffrey said, grudgingly.

They ate in silence while Jeffrey, always making sure to give the large man the smaller of the portions, devoured his find.

After everything on the plate had been eaten, the man spoke, softly, but carefully.

"I'm not from around here," the man said, "But you can call me Ike."

"I'm Jeffrey."

"Good to meet you Jeffrey, and thank you for sharing your meal."

"Yea, no problem. I wasn't really gonna hurt you, I just wanted to make sure you weren't gonna steal my food." Jeffrey said.

"I've never stolen anything in my life," Ike said, as he massaged his hands.

"What do you do for food then?" Jeffrey asked.

"I usually just work for it. Everybody needs something moved, or someone worked over."

"You're a hitman?"

"Nah, just someone who does jobs that nobody else wants to do." Ike said. There was no remorse in his voice.

"Nobody messes with ya cause you're so big, eh?" Jeffrey leaned back against the building's wall, propping his arms up on his knees.

"Nah, nobody messes with me cause I can do things to them… Bad things."

"Me and you should stick together," Jeffrey decided, "We could be like a team or something."

"I don't know," Ike looked down at his palms, dirty and scarred. "Most people who are around me end up getting hurt."

"I can hold my own." Jeffrey puffed out his chest.

"No doubt!" Ike said, with a hint of a smile.

"So why are you here?" Jeffrey asked.

"Just traveling through, helping people who need helping."

Ike stood up, and stretched his arms. The sleeves of his trench coat slid up his arms revealing a multitude of tattoos. There was only one recognizable to Jeffrey, the king of hearts. The rest of the tattoos were an assortment of symbols and characters. They looked like some kind of weird language that he didn't know. Ike noticed Jeffrey looking at his arms and quickly covered them up.

"What's all those tattoos mean?"

"Nothing much," Ike replied, "Just some reminders to keep me on track."

Ike turned and started to walk away, his trench coat trailing on the wind behind him.

Jeffrey called out. "Hey Ike! Where you going?"

"Nowhere special." Ike shrugged.

Ike then stopped, turned his head and look at Jeffrey out of the corner of his eye. "You going to be okay kid?"

"I've survived on these streets so far, eh?" Jeffrey gave him a smirk, proud of his accomplishment.

"I tell ya what kid," Ike paused. "You stick with me and I'll make sure nobody messes with you."

Stunned, Jeffrey mulled the concept over in his head. Ike hadn't tried to hurt him, didn't ask for anything, but was very intimidating. Jeffrey could do much worse than have a friend like Ike. Actually Jeffrey couldn't really ask for a better bodyguard than Ike. Seemed like he had taken a liking to Jeffrey, and was one of the few people who had actually acknowledged him as a person, and not some street rat that needed to be put out of its misery.

"Okay fine," Jeffrey said, "I'll be *your* bodyguard. But only under one condition."

"Ha," Ike chuckled, "What's that?"

"I want some tats like yours." Jeffrey said, with resolve.

"Hmm, maybe you should know what these 'tats' mean first." Ike started to walk away again.

Jeffrey ran to catch up and started walking just in front of him, giving Ike enough distance to feel *safe* with Jeffrey's protection.

"Maybe you should tell me. I don't want to get a mistake permanently etched on my skin," Jeffrey said.

Ike stopped, pulled one sleeve up and starred at his bare arm closely and hesitated before he spoke. "These are a mistake, but not the kind you're talking about."

"Wha?" Jeffrey cocked his head, his face scrunched.

"These are rune etchings." Ike traced the lines of one of the symbols on his arm with his finger.

"Rune etchings? Like magic stuff?" Jeffrey stopped, crossed his arms, and looked at Ike.

"Yea, something like that." Ike brushed his sleeve back down his arm.

Ike started walking down the street again, passing Jeffrey as the boy stood there looking confused. Jeffrey snapped to attention and had to run to catch up with him, since every step of Ike's was at least two steps for Jeffrey.

"I still want one," Jeffrey said. "Where can I get one like that?"

"I can give you one of mine," Ike scoffed, "But you may not like the weight of it."

"You think I'm a wimp, don't you."

Ike raised an eyebrow. "Not at all, kid."

After a long silent walk, Ike stopped in front of a building and squatted down on the steps with his hands clasped and his arms resting on his knees.

"Here's the deal, kid." Ike looked up at Jeffrey.

"I was once like you. Young... Scrappy... Homeless... And lonely..." Ike swallowed hard with the last word.

"But I found something that kept me going, gave me hope and more importantly, gave me heart." A quiet solemnness spread across Ike's face.

This was the first time Jeffrey saw Ike. Really saw him. Saw the pain. Saw the loneliness. Saw the years of sadness.

"I'm tired Jeffrey." Ike confessed. "I'm tired of this responsibility, of this life. I just want to go home."

"Why don't you go home then?" Jeffrey said.

"It's not that simple," Ike said. "I have to find a replacement."

"Maybe I can help you find 'em." Jeffrey puffed out his chest again.

"You have no idea how much that means to me." Ike leaned back on the steps resting his elbows on the top landing. Looked up into the sky, lost in thought, focusing on the dark clouds starting to form above the city. A city that would start waking up soon, beginning its daily grind. He leaned forward and stared at Jeffrey.

"Are you ready, kid?"

"Sure." Jeffrey said, slightly offended.

"Are you?" Ike's voice was mocking.

"Look," Jeffrey said. "You showed up out of nowhere and I shared my meal with you. You asked if I wanted to follow you, and I said yes. All I did was ask you about your tattoos and you started getting all weird and telling me all this stuff about once being like me. I told you, I'm ready. Either believe it or not, doesn't matter to me, but I'm tired too! Tired of being the runt. Tired of having to fight for my food. Tired of not having a place to sleep at night. Tired of being pushed around by everyone! And I'm starting to get tired of you!"

Ike, taken back by this sudden confrontation

looked to his left, looked to his right, and saw that the coast was clear of any pedestrians.

"Very well." Ike motioned for Jeffrey to sit next to him on the steps. "This won't take long."

He pulled up the sleeves of his coat, and as his hands started moving in strange rotations in front of him, rain started to fall. It was a gentle rain, washing the streets before them. Running down the gutters of the building behind them. Gushing onto the streets and eventually into the sewer grates.

Jeffrey watched Ike, completely entranced by what was happening next to him. Ike's hands moved in slow methodical patterns, his fingers bending and turning, making different shapes and symbols in midair. Faster and faster his hands moved, blurring the lines of where his hands ended and the orb of energy began. Growing larger than the encompassing boundary of his hands, he quickly threw his hands to the left and right allowing the orb to completely engulf them, shielding the falling rain and allowing Jeffrey to see out through the glistening sheath of the orb.

"What in the world…" Jeffrey whispered.

"This world is not my home," Ike sing-songed. "I'm just a passin' through."

Ike stood up, took one hand and smoothed it

down across the surface of his arm, as if he was wiping something off of it. The runes and symbols tattooed on his arm came off as if cleaning a blackboard of its chalk. He held out the arm that was now void of the markings, beckoning Jeffrey to extend and lend his arm to him. Ike took his other hand, the one that had cleared the symbols, and proceeded to scan his hand across Jeffrey's arm. The ink slowly started to appear on Jeffrey's blank arm like a canvas or a tapestry. Ike repeated the process with his other arm, transferring the ancient symbols over to Jeffrey.

Jeffrey, wasn't completely sure what he was getting into, but decided that the resulting power he started to feel was worth the consequences. Not only was he being filled with an overwhelming sense of power, but also with a sense of dread and despair.

"I don't understand," Jeffrey said shaking his head. "I don't understand."

"You told me you were ready, and told me you meant it." Ike replied.

"What did you *do* to me?" Jeffrey asked.

"I gave you what you *wanted*," Ike replied, "I gave you power, and now it's time for me to go home."

Ike turned and started to walk through the bubble shaped orb they were surrounded by, crooked his head back towards Jeffrey and said, "You have immense power, but you're still young. You must learn to harness the gift that's been given to you."

"What are you talking about?" Jeffrey asked. "I don't understand."

"You'll soon find out," Ike said. "Oh, and one last thing. Those runes. As long as they're part of you, you'll never die."

With his last remark, Ike stepped fully through the membrane of the orb and Jeffrey could see the hazy-figured outline of Ike walking down the grassy hill on the other side, into a bright other world. Jeffrey jumped up and ran, trying to catch up with Ike, only to discover that when he stepped through the barrier, he found himself back on the dark, dirty streets of a city, unaware of what had transpired between them.

Jeffrey fell to his knees, his arms and hands lay open across his lap. Staring down at the runes, etched and now part of him, glistening in the early light of the day. Tears streamed from his eyes, mixing with rain as it cascaded down from his dirty hair.

Jeffrey's body reacted before he even knew what was happening. His hands had instinctively shot up and crossed in front of his head and body to form a defensive shield. He heard tires screeching.

He lowered his hands and the wreckage directly

in front of him didn't make sense, it looked as though the car had slammed right into a brick wall. The front of it crumpled, its fluids pouring out creating a cocktail of petroleum and acid.

Jeffrey stood, taking in the whole scene. The driver was slumped over his steering wheel, blood was on the inside of the broken windshield, and a blaring horn gave up its last breath. Light began to dance around the wrecked mechanical beast as fire lapped up the fumes from the fuel that leaked out. Jeffrey panicked and wanted to run away.

Something was different about him this time. His mind screamed to run, but his legs stood firm and planted. Arguing internally between his mind and body, Jeffrey finally gave in to the urge. He walked around to the driver's side door, fire escaping for its life from beneath each step he took. He grabbed hold of the handle and pulled. The door didn't budge, and he inadvertently broke the handle off. He didn't let that stop him. Sliding his hands around the door frame, he discovered a few gaps large enough to grab onto. With a sudden jerk of his newly found muscles, Jeffrey managed to pull the door out of its feeble framing. The driver was lifeless. *This is too easy*, Jeffrey thought to himself.

Jeffrey committed to giving in to his primal urge

and reached in, undid the seat belt and grabbed the driver by his coat and lifted him through the opening he created in the side of the car.

Jeffrey, watching from a distance, saw the response teams converge on the scene of the wreckage. He watched as they put out what was left of the fire. He watched as they searched for the cause of the wreckage. He watched as they loaded up the still breathing driver into the back of the ambulance.

He looked down at his arms and saw the runes glowing as their power coursed through his body healing the parts of him burnt by the fire, the bones broken from the impact, and the lacerations from tearing the door off its hinges. The power that surged through his body did one more thing: it gave him a sense of duty, a sense of pride, and a reason to live. Forever.

DESTINY

A. B. ALVAREZ

Everyone has felt that pull. The one that hints at greater things. The one that says There is More to Life Than This. That one in a million person, that one in a billion, that feels the tug and has to do something about it. Has to scratch that itch. What if you were the answer to someone else's itch?

The mountain rose before me while I wondered if what I was doing would go down as a feat of human endurance or just the idiotic behavior of a man looking for something that didn't exist. Idiotic I felt; it would probably be carved on my tombstone if they ever found my body. Human endurance? That was a given since all I had done since I arrived in Timbuktu was hitch rides and walk to the summit of Mount Halukutu.

The location was random. I didn't really know where to start. What I did know was that my journey here was one filled with despair. Or at least a few good jokes.

At the airport in London the customs agents looked at my itinerary and thought I was a climber. The questions were predictable. "Are you sure you know what you're getting yourself into?"

"I am bound by law to notify you that if anything goes wrong or occurs in spite of warnings to the contrary you will be on your own."

Well that was a feeling I had had for a long time.

"Dad," my son Artemis asked, "what if you don't come back?"

"I'll be back," I assured him even as I knew that the odds were good I was lying to him.

"Honey," my wife asked, "you know I want you to do what you think is right, but," she would never complete that sentence as she walked out the door with my son, a few suitcases she had packed in the car and my past. I had given everything I had been to them: husband, father, provider. The future me stood by the rather simple white door of our New Jersey apartment and watched them leave. The hallway was normally quite bright, but setting the scene was a thunderstorm of biblical proportions that would dissipate as soon as they drove away but would stay in my soul forever.

Then I had prepared myself, a non-athletic, non-climber, social climber, with what little I could find on Google and what little my overdrawn credit card could sustain. I didn't touch my savings. That was for the ones I'd left behind.

Being left behind was something I had a lot of experience with.

Climbing a mountain is a rather interesting thing to do. All humans at one time or other have experienced the thrill of wanting to climb a hill, or monkey bars, or rocks. The majority of folks, the ones who grow up, who micro-evolve into the writhing mass of washed humanity, give up that feeling. Others pursue it with a passion most will never understand (is it passion? Or self-destruction?). I am doing it, the act of climbing, of pursuing, for an answer.

It was morning. The partially sun-covered sky hovered over me. The temperature was chilly and promised to get colder as the day wore on. Was I ready for this?

No.

Hell, yes.

Continuing to walk with my thick cotton-lined pants, heavy duty boots, and light coat I began walking over the bare ground where sprouts of green were all around, but so little that you would think you were in another world. In a place where the rest of humanity had simply forgotten. Maybe it had.

I thought I saw a glint of something high above me. Was that it? Was I already seeing things? Did it matter? I thought of my lucky three of diamonds. Three glints.

The thing about going about something alone is that the only person you can blame is yourself. Given my life, there was plenty of blame to go around. The wind brushed against my face and the chill raced down my spine. Tonight was going to be murder. Maybe literally.

The rocks, those random chunks of earth scattered all around, sitting on the hard, dusty ground became more numerous as I proceeded forward. The going was rough, but this was not K2 or Everest. This was a place that might as well be Area 51. A place everyone knew existed, but no one ever journeyed to.

Why was I? Maybe the joke was on me. I had been doing some research, something I always enjoyed when I was in school and at work when given the opportunity, which wasn't often. That moment I can only describe as my Close Encounter moment: something about a photograph in the journal of a climber long dead, at a location long lost, filled me with a desire to discover, investigate, wander. I didn't know the questions, but my brain knew I had to find an answer. An answer akin to Life, the Universe, and Everything, but one that pulled at my head for rationale and my heart for motivation.

The picture was a standard sort. The members of a climbing team standing at their basecamp at the foot of a nondescript location holding something that looked like...I can't describe it. All I know was this amorphous blob they held flipped a switch through my eyes into my brain and turned the volume up to 11. That night I packed my things, tried to leave, said good-bye to family, and instead they said good-bye to me.

Something about the last straw.

It was getting dark. I didn't stop that often, but after a week of hitching rides and going down roads less traveled I was at a point in my energy where stopping was the only way for me to keep going. I looked behind me every so often. The road down looked sketchy. Did I really just climb all that? Did I really just spend the last few weeks working my way here? Dark was settling on everything. I pulled out my last bottle of water, only half-full, and drank a few drops. Once it was done it would be done.

Was I worried that I would die from dehydration or starvation? No. I knew that the journey would end and I would somehow work things out. I wasn't Ernest Shackleton, a man with luck and balls to match, but I was resourceful. Didn't I save the company a few million dollars a few years back before they decided that I had not done the same often enough or soon enough to merit a consideration before being laid off (which is corporate-speak for fired)?

Was it snowing? Darkness was all around me. I stopped. I leaned against a rock, but it was too cold. I lay down on the ground and, using my backpack as a pillow, fell asleep. It wouldn't get so cold that I had to worry about freezing to death, but I did need to conserve what little heat and passion I had to start again in the morning.

When would I start? Time didn't mean anything at this point either. I would move when I could see before my eyes.

I blinked and found myself on my way at first light. My back hurt.

The glint I had seen the day before was gone. I thought I had seen it in the darkest part of the night, but what light would have bounced off it? Maybe it was giving off light? Was it a beacon?

Whatever. If my eyes were playing tricks they were welcome. I had been on my own for so long that I wondered what I would have been like with a companion.

It was later that afternoon that I saw the shadow trailing behind me.

I don't mean my own shadow, or the shadows of the rocks (perhaps), but the shadowy outline of a figure making its way up behind me. The view around me was exalting. The sky so bright in the morning, cloudy at various parts of the day creating a shadowless landscape, and the dark skies in the evening were all I knew. The sweat running down my back felt chill. The pit of my lower back felt like a small frozen pool. As the day drew to a close I sat on the sharp edge of a smallish boulder and sighed.

The figure pulled up next to me.

"Took a bit to catch up."

"Yes." The words were stuck in my mouth. There was no saliva left to let them slide out into the world. I didn't think I would need to ever do that again. I looked away and stared up towards my goal. Getting closer, but still so far.

"I saw you in the distance and thought I would join you."

"Good," I replied. I let myself down from the boulder as slowly as I could, the soles of my feet sore from the never-ending walk across the surface of a planet I was only now realizing I barely knew, and lay down and fell asleep.

The next morning as we walked towards our goal, our light at the end of the metaphorical tunnel, I turned to my companion and just look at his face. He didn't seem familiar.

"Don't waste your energy looking at me. Just keep walking."

I nodded. Good advice. The air was getting thinner.

The top of the mountain tantalizingly far moments ago approached faster and faster. Maybe we would arrive today. Maybe I would be able to answer the new question in my mind. The question that perhaps brings us all to the same place somewhere in our journeys through life: what does it mean?

At least I hadn't built a to-scale replica of Devil's Point in my living room. Maybe that would have been enough. Maybe I wouldn't be out here in the cold pulling myself up the side of rock.

Maybe, maybe, maybe.

Shut up.

"I'll be fine. Just keep going," my companion said. The figure wore full climbing gear and a new warm coat, gloves, and boots. We pulled ourselves up onto a large outcropping that could support us both and we looked out onto the world surrounding us.

"If I didn't know better I'd say you're here looking for what I'm looking for," the figure said.

I nodded. I felt out of words.

"You're looking for the answer." He turned himself toward me. "Not just any answer. The answer."

I shivered. If I thought I could steal his coat I might have. The temperature was dropping and I was starting to fear that I would turn into a statue nearing the summit and never get to the top. The top where the goal lay.

The answer.

"When we get to the next outcrop I'll let you have my coat. You'll be fine."

I shivered, nodded, stood and kept going. I heard the crunching of his boots on the air and snow that surrounded us with a purity akin to zeal.

Wearing my companion's coat, but still feeling the cold we came upon a chunk of steel sticking out of the ground. I made to touch it, but my companion warned me against it.

"If your hand sticks to the metal you're liable to cut open your skin to let go. Not a good idea."

Not a good idea? Was this trip, this final journey as far as I could tell, a good idea?

"Of course, it is. You just want to know."

I needed to know. I needed to know. The words were an echo in my head.

I nodded again as the wind whipped around me like frozen spider web tendrils. I shivered uncontrollably and I sat next to the extruded piece of manmade hardware. If it was manmade how did it get up here?

"Best question I've heard from you since we met up. How indeed?"

I shivered and closed my eyes. Would I be able to open them later? I didn't know or care. Exhaustion made the decision and I was just following along now.

I turned over on my side to get my arms under me to I could push myself up. I was wearing the gloves of my companion though the cold cutting through the palms of my hands and my knees felt as raw as if I weren't wearing them at all.

"You'll be fine. The cold cuts through everything. If you believe you can make it, you will."

Belief. Of course, I just had to believe and everything would be alright. I would tap my ruby slippers together and say "There's no place like home." No, it should be "There's no place like here." Where was here?

I walked about the metal chunks. Was there something I could make out from it? A shape, a use, something I could just hold onto as a piece of reality in the midst of this terrible cold?

Whatever it was had collided with the ground at a high rate of speed. I saw a flash of memory of (something?) coming at the ground as fast as it could and exploding on contact. Vibrations (was I feeling vibrations?) emanated from the wreckage. Was I vibrating along with it? Was there some sort of resonant frequency I was attuned to?

What the hell was I talking about?

"Just a little further. It's getting colder and you can finally sit in the warmth."

There was warmth ahead? It was snowing. If I had a beard I suspect I would have looked like the explorers of old. Shackleton, eat your heart out. You might have survived Antarctica, but I am going to survive and make sure that we are saved.

We? Saved?

I shook my head. My companion was gone.

"It's okay," he said. "We're almost there."

I ignored the figure. I knew we were almost there. I could feel the resonance. Could feel the vibrations, the visions. I knew where I was supposed to go, where I was supposed to be.

I moved my legs as fast as they could go which didn't amount to much, but I saw what now seems like what I had known all along, but I couldn't have until I was close enough to feel, close enough to touch, close enough to die.

The crushed outer compartment of something sat at the summit of the mountain. Snow covered everything and the sound of the wind dug into my ears like someone was crushing my ear while poking it with a hot instrument.

"Enter the code." I looked to my right and there

was the figure again.

I nodded and touched a panel to the right of something that looked like a doorway with a pattern best left to the dreamers or the stupid. I didn't really see any outline of a door. I just knew it was there. It wasn't part of the mountain yet jutted out as if it is had been placed there by a giant who simply shoved it into the ground enough to anchor it, but not enough to bury it.

It looked like the entrance to a bomb shelter covered with snow. The wind blew dry air into my nose along with tiny glass shards of snow. The door opened and I stepped inside.

The figure led me into a corridor that contained just enough light for me to see by, but not enough for the detail I would normally expect when entering some place as ominous as the shelter. Pipes appeared to be hanging from the ceiling while grey drab walls led deeper into the dark abyss. The floor was tilted enough that I slid every few steps as I stepped downward into my future.

Was I walking fast or slow? It was so hard to tell. Every step sent sharp stabs of pain up my legs. The figure waved at me. *Follow me. This way.* What could I do?

I blinked.

I stood before a chair. The figure gently took my hands and led me onto the full cushioned softness with a warmth that felt comfortable and welcoming. I felt myself melt into the material that I could not tell was vinyl or leather or plastic. I looked down. The coat I thought I had been wearing was not a coat. I was in my clothes from earlier. There were holes across my chest like large black freckles. My skin was frost bitten. My shoes had split and part of the soles had given up. My feet, peeking through the gap between the shoe and the sole contained black splotches.

The chair tilted back. I closed my eyes. Perhaps I could sleep.

"I have been waiting for you." A voice in my mind, caressing my face.

I knew you were.

"If you had not arrived soon there would have been no notifier."

I know.

"You answered the call. You are the new notifier."

The new notifier.

"When the procedure is over you will take over. I will disengage."

I'll be warm.

"Yes, you will."

A panel appeared before my eyes. I wasn't sure what I was looking at, but I knew I would be looking at it for a long time.

"Yes, you will."

Bands crisscrossed my chest, legs, arms and wrists.

"Notify us. Only you will know when."

Only I will know.

Two circular blades came out of the back of the chair and cut my head off.

My head was lifted and placed on a pedestal. I couldn't see around it, but I knew that it was high enough that I would be able to see what was needed to be seen. I felt a mesh embedded in the back of my head so I could control what I needed to control.

I felt woozy and then the blood began flowing again.

My vision cleared. I could see the panel monitoring the skies for thousands of miles.

I felt the need to be cautious.

I knew what I needed to do.

I would know when to let them know.

I would notify them. I knew who they were.

This was my destiny.

DIAMANTÉE

JESSE R. LYLE

Stealing is wrong and what if the consequences could change your life, inside and out?

The bullet sound rang through the alley as Becky ducked behind the pile of broken pallets. She'd escaped from one terrifying situation only to find herself in another.

How am I going to get outta here?

Bullets zinged past, sounding like angry yellow jackets, above her head, ricocheting off the walls of the alley around her. She had nowhere to go, and this hiding place wasn't going to last much longer. They knew where she was and they were coming for her.

She clutched the box she'd stolen from the compound, but she'd had no idea they would pick up her scent so quickly and would aim to kill. There was a whole lot more going on here than just some rent-a-cop security guards chasing her. Apparently, there was something more precious in this box she held than she'd realized. She hadn't been briefed on what it was, just that it could fetch a hefty sum to the right fence.

The barricade of old pallets wouldn't hide her for much longer. Several men were shouting as they searched for her. She thought she could make out at least six different voices. She couldn't pinpoint the accents, but how would that help her right now anyway? This box wasn't worth it, whatever it might be. It just wasn't worth dying over.

There was a lull in the bullets whizzing around her, and she took the opportunity to shout out, "STOP! I GIVE UP!"

"Come out from behind the pallets slowly," a voice said, in the distance.

"I'll give you the box, just please don't shoot me!" she said.

"Step out from behind the pallets," The voice said again.

I'm going to die. I'm going to step out from behind these pallets and they're going to shoot me, dead. I just know it.

"If I come out, do you promise not to hurt me?"

"Step out from behind the pallets."

What is up with this guy? Sounds like a broken record.

"Great, Becky…" She said, under her breath. "You just *had* to swipe this box didn't you, you just had to overhear them talking about it, and you just *had* to get it yourself, didn't you?"

"Step out from behind the pallets!"

"What are you going to do girl?" she asked herself. "How are you going to get out of this one?"

"If you will step out from behind the pallets, we promise not to shoot you," the voice said, but it sounded a little closer this time. "But you've gotta come out now or we *will* kill you."

"Alright, alright, alright…" Becky said.

Holding the box in one hand, she put her hands up as high as she could and started to walk out from behind the only protection in the alley. The lights someone trained on her location blinded her and made it difficult to see anything but dark silhouettes everywhere. She heard movement and saw the rough shapes starting to converge on her location.

She heard a zing, something like a firecracker, go past her head. She heard the dull thud of lead hitting soft tissue as one by one the rough shadows in front of her slumped over and fell to the ground.

The figures looked odd doubling over while the curious zing, thud, zing, thud, zipped past her over and over again. Then something pulled her down behind the pallets. She hugged the ground while a barrage of bullets flew back and forth. She was in a daze. Smelling the burned aroma of gunpowder and the thickness of iron rich blood in the air made it hard to gather her thoughts.

What was going on?

"Are you okay?" A voice yelled into her ear over the loud volley above them.

"Yeah, I think so," she replied.

"Good," the strong voice said. "We've gotta move."

"Where?" she asked. "I didn't see anywhere I could go."

The figure grabbed her around the waist and dragged her over to the closest wall, shielded by a small buildout of bricks towering to the sky. He attached something around her waist and tugged on a tether hanging next to the wall. She felt the pull of strength and the rhythm of a winch tugging her upward. She reached the top and felt strong arms pull her over the edge onto the flat roof.

"Who are you?" she cried out.

"Go! Go! Go!" a large man wearing body armor and tactical gear yelled as he unhooked her and shoved her towards a woman perched on the opposite corner of the building.

"Follow her!" the man yelled and pointed towards the woman.

He turned, grabbed his submachine gun, and took aim in the direction of where she had unnaturally taken flight from the ground.

Becky didn't know how she got to the opposite corner of the building, but figured her legs must have carried her there, if for no other reason than they just wanted to get away from the sounds of gunshots echoing up from the alley below.

Becky reached the woman who quickly handed her a harness. The woman was thin and wore black tactical gear, but wasn't wearing the bulky body armor the larger man was wearing. Instead she wore goggles that had a faint hint of green glowing from around the seal that was affixed to the woman's face. The woman kept scanning the area below and around them.

"We've gotta move girl," she said.

"Where do we have to go?" Becky fumbled putting the harness on.

"We're going to get you out of here, away from those people trying to kill you. Do you still have the package?" the woman in black said.

"Yes, I've still got it." Becky secured her harness and showed the woman the box. Her hands were shaking. "What's this all about?"

"We'll explain later, but for now, do not, under any circumstance, let go of that package," the woman said.

Becky pulled the box close against her chest. With everything happening so fast all around her, the one thing she had control over was holding onto the box.

"Step up here," The woman gestured to the ledge she stood on. "We need to go."

Becky stepped up, and felt the woman attach a line to her harness. She gave it tug, made sure it was secured, and then did the same with hers.

Becky's eyes reflected the feeling in her stomach, "What are we about ready to do…"

"Have you ever been zip-lining before?" the woman asked.

"Once," Becky replied.

"Well… it's kind of like that, except we'll be moving too fast to use gloves, we'll be letting gravity slow us down. But don't worry, there's a net at the end that'll catch you. Just make sure to hold onto that package. It'll all be for nothing if we don't get you and that package to the landing zone." The woman in black attached both of their lines to the steel cable above their heads.

"Wait a minute...," Becky said.

"Just remember to breathe and don't let go. The harness will do the rest." The woman shoved Becky off the ledge.

Becky remember the one time she had zip-lined, the thrill of quickly falling, but still feeling like she had a little bit of control since she had used thick leather gloves on the line above her that would help slow her down if she felt she was going too fast. At that moment all she knew that the ground was coming up to meet her way too fast.

What felt like an eternity only lasted for a couple of seconds as the harness snagged her and she felt the rush of wind blowing past her as it carried her horizontally now instead of free-falling to the ground. She felt her speed increase, faster and faster. The harness was taking her to some unknown location, and she was helplessly along for the ride. She sailed past several buildings in the darkness, coming a little too close for comfort a couple of times. Obediently during the whole trip she never let go of the box.

She knew she must be getting to the end since the

slack in the line allowed her to slow some, but the sudden feel of the rope net catching her still gave her a shock. The woman in black came in fast too, but somehow made it look effortless as she expertly controlled her body. She pulled her linchpin and dropped just before plowing into Becky and rolled gracefully out of the net.

Becky struggled to get out of the net even with a couple people holding it. She finally got to her feet, a little wobbly and weak from all the blood rushing to the back of her head, and tried to focus on just standing upright and not looking like a complete amateur.

"This way," the woman said, motioning for Becky to follow her.

"Hold on." Becky stumbled in the direction where the woman motioned.

They entered what looked like a makeshift command center. A tall muscular man wearing a black beret stopped his conversation with another man and came over to greet Becky.

"Welcome, Becky." His voice was deep and rough.

"Uh, hi?" Becky looked to the woman in black for guidance.

"I'm General Peterson, and this is my temporary

command central. It's good to finally meet you," he said.

"I'd like to say the same," Becky said, "but I'm really confused right now. Don't get me wrong, I'm happy you guys saved me and all, but I'm ready for this night to be over."

"I don't blame you," General Peterson said. "And we'll get you debriefed and on your way soon enough. It's good to see that you still have the package."

"Yeah, but I'm still not even sure what it is." She held the box out to him.

"Oh, no," Peterson put his hands behind his back, "I can't touch that. In fact, none of us can. You're the only one. That's why we transported you here."

"Uh, besides the point of you knowing that I had it, what is it?" Becky held it as far away from her body as possible. A plague in a seemingly harmless container.

"It's actually a prototype, cleverly disguised as a very common object," the General said, "Go ahead and open it."

Becky reluctantly brought the box closer to her chest and started looking it over. It was simple in design, but well made with importance on the quality of the construction itself. She found a recessed locking mechanism and slowly pushed it.

Everyone in the room had been silent once they saw her enter the command center, and now they took a few steps back away from her, almost as if they were ready for the box to explode and she wasn't in on the joke.

With the lock disengaged, she gulped the frog residing in her throat, placed her hand over the lid and grasped it. The General put his hand on top of hers.

"No one else can open this box except for you. But if you open it, it will most certainly change your life forever." General Peterson said.

"Talk about some heavy stuff," Becky said. "What the heck is in this thing?"

"Something with immense power and something that will make your life mean something. I have no idea what the object will look like, but whatever it is, it's meant for you." he said.

Becky took a deep breath, and thought about what her life had meant up till this moment. It wasn't much. She was ordinary. This kind of thing didn't happen to her. This kind of thing wasn't *supposed* to happen to her. Why her? Why now? She thought back to the last few minutes of her night: the thrill of fighting, running across roof tops, being part of something bigger.

And she liked it.

I'm tired of not doing anything that matters.

She opened the lid of the box expecting a big fanfare, but there wasn't a big release of air or smoke. There were no disco lights bouncing out of it. There wasn't any kind of big show. Instead, what she saw was a single simple playing card. The eight of diamonds.

"What kind of joke is this?" Becky said looking up to the General.

He wasn't laughing. Instead he was looking at the card intently.

"Interesting," he said. "Go ahead. Pick it up."

"Okay," she said reluctantly.

Becky picked up the seemingly normal playing card. It felt warm when she touched it and she felt an overwhelming urge to not let go. The graphics on the card liquefied and swirled. The red gel-like liquid traveled to her finger tips and engulfed her hand climbed up her arm. The red gel coating, unbiased in its travel, eventually covered her entire body, sank into her skin and became transparent.

Becky set the box down and stared at her arms and legs. She touched her arm. She felt her skin, but something was different. She smacked her arm. This time she didn't feel her skin. She felt a barrier;

something rigid. Small translucent diamonds rippled on the surface of her skin out and away from the area she hit.

"It didn't hurt." She struck her arm over and over, conjuring up the same results.

"I'm not sure what's going on here," The General said, "but you appear to be the owner of an ultra-lightweight and transparent body armor. How do you feel?"

"I feel...Great!" Smiling, Becky touched her arms, legs, and face.

The woman in black stepped forward holding a paper printout. "Excuse me, General," she said and handed it to Peterson. "Her code name."

General Peterson gave the paper a quick look and smiled. "Appropriate." Peterson looked at Becky. "Your code name is *Diamantée.*"

"As long as, you know, you're covered in diamonds anyway," The woman in black said.

Diamantée. I like it. Becky felt a level of pride and purpose she hadn't known in a long time.

SLIT BY THREE

DEREK E. MILLER

I've always loved street performers, especially those in New Orleans. I've always loved tales of secret agents. What if the two worlds collided?

It was imposing and humbling. Richard stared at the 129 stars on the wall. Some of the stars were referenced in the book of honor below them with some names that were so secret their star was blank. Looking at the memorial honoring those who had died in the service of the CIA kept one in a type of holy trance.

Richard stood in CIA headquarters wondering why in the world he was here of all places on planet earth. He truly had no idea why. Was he in some sort of trouble? Was he involved with something he shouldn't be?

He was a simple street magician hustler. Making his money picking pockets, card tricks, and pulling quarters from behind kids' ears. People walking by loved his act and would throw money in the hat at his feet. But what really got people's attention was his ability to throw cards at a dart board hitting it dead center every time.

Three days ago he was performing in New Orleans when a man dropped a business card in the hat he laid out for tips. It wasn't until lunch time that Richard pulled the money out and found the business card.

All that was on it was the CIA symbol, a street address, and the time *3:00 p.m.*

Obviously this had to be a joke. Was this some sort of invitation? The address wasn't too far from where Richard hustled tourists. Why not walk by later that day?

At 2:30 p.m. Richard packed up his bag of tricks and walked to the address. He expected men in black with earpieces standing outside the door or for a water balloon to fall on his head. All that was there was a wooden door. Instead of knocking he just turned the old brass knob and the door opened.

In the middle of the room was a woman sitting behind a huge old desk.

"Welcome Richard. Your flight leaves in two hours. Here is your plane ticket and two thousand dollars in cash for your time and anything you need along the way. You'd better get going. There's a car out front that will drive you to the airport."

"What is this and why am I going to Washington D.C.?"

"Sir, all I can tell you is you are expected in D.C. in a few hours."

"What if I refuse?"

"You won't refuse. This will pay more than you can dream of and if you don't go how will you take care of your family with that new tumor your doctor just told you about?"

Richard was speechless for a moment. It was only last week that his doctor gave him the horrific news. A time bomb in his brain.

Richard could sense that he wouldn't get anything more out of her.

"Thank you for the ticket and money."

"Car is outside. You don't want to keep your driver waiting."

Richard turned and went out the door and into the waiting car.

Upon landing two men holding a mini whiteboard with his last name written on it waited for him. As they drove away from D.C. the men never spoke a word. Eventually, Richard saw CIA headquarters. Passing through a check point they parked and walked into building.

Richard had watched enough TV to know what CIA headquarters looked like. Was he in trouble?

He was asked to wait for a few minutes in the lobby. It was here that he first saw the Memorial Wall.

It did not seem long until another man in a white shirt and khakis came out and asked for Richard to follow him. After walking through boring hallways and switching floors in a standard elevator, he was ushered into a dimly lit room. Eight people sat at a long table waiting for him.

"Why am I here?" Richard asked.

"Sorry for the cloak and dagger stuff. You are not in any trouble, but we need you to do something for us."

"You had my attention at two thousand dollars. Who are you?"

A deck of cards slid over to him on the table and

a shooting range paper target of a man dropped down on the far side of the room.

"Just call me Bob, please take a card and see if you can hit the target."

"Huh?"

"It's simple. Please take a card out and try and hit the throat of the man on the target."

"Sure, but usually I get a tip for that trick. The two grand paid for my time to come here."

A twenty dollar bill was slid down the table.

Richard opened the pack of cards and with lightning speed threw 52 cards at the head of the target. Not one missed. The target was nothing more than shredded paper by the time he got done.

"Want to see it again?" he asked.

Another pack of cards was slide down the table.

"These are a bit heavier," Richard said, as he hefted the package.

Another twenty dollar bill slid down the table.

A new target came from the floor. This one was not paper. It was a manikin of a man.

"Please throw your cards again. But be careful, these cards are a little more dangerous." Bob said.

Richard opened the pack and his fingers felt the cards. They were indeed a touch heavier.

A cut formed on his ring finger as it slid across an edge. Blood formed on the three of spades.

"Be careful. You can slice your finger off in a New York second if you're not careful." Bob said.

"What material is this?" Richard asked.

"Don't worry about that. Please, demonstrate your ability to throw your card and take off the head of the target."

Richard grabbed the card in the way he had trained himself with years of practice, expecting the card to stick into the target.

He threw the three of spades and instead of the card striking the manikin it sliced completely through the target half removing the head.

"What the heck?" Richard asked.

"Excellent, they work as promised." Bob said.

"What is the point of all this?" Richard asked.

"Richard, we have a problem and we think you are our man to take care of it."

"And that is what?"

The lights in the room brightened and now Richard could see in the room. He saw the faces of the men and women.

"What I'm about to tell you is currently one of the most guarded secrets in the world and even I can't tell you everything." Bob said.

"Just tell me." Richard asked.

"Have you heard of Huan Juan the Third? Bob asked.

"Yeah, that nut bag ruler who tortures his own people." Richard said.

"To get straight to the point, he has developed a serum that could destroy the world as we know it. I can't tell you what it does except there is only one in the world right now. If he can get this mass produced it will be devastating. No one has been able to get a sample of this serum." Bob said.

"And I can help how?" Richard asked.

"Turns out he is a fan of magic. He is holding a celebration and is inviting magicians from around the world. Any big names are turning him down for obvious reasons. They don't want to be seen entertaining a madman for money. However some no name magicians can get invited and they don't have to worry about their reputations. No offence." Bob said.

"None taken. It's not like he's caught my show on the streets of New Orleans." Richard said.

"We can make sure he gets info on you and get you an invite. While there we need you to kill him." Bob said.

"I don't think so." Richard said.

"I'm telling you the world is at stake." Bob said.

"It's a suicide mission." Richard said

"Aren't you dead already?" Bob said.

"Didn't know my tumor was the talk of the town." Richard said.

"We have people on the inside but no one can get close enough to him physically or with a weapon. He has that one vial with him at all times. Like its nuclear launch codes or something. However, an item as basic as a deck of cards can be snuck in, and with your ability to throw a card with such deadly accuracy. Finally someone can kill him. In the chaos you can escape and we can grab the box with the vial in it." Bob said.

"It's crazy." Richard said.

"Yes. And so is he." Bob said.

"I'm not doing it unless I know what this vial is. I'm not releasing a virus in the air or something stupid like that. Richard said.

One of the women around the table leaned forward. "Just tell him."

Bob took a deep breath. "We don't know how he did it but he has been able to create a serum to have a person live forever. If they are shot thirty times, they will heal and live forever. If they have a tumor it would be cured. We lost five agents that brought out the data."

"If there is only one shot, how do you know this? Richard asked.

"There were two created. He's already taken one of them. It took immense resources and manpower to create. The news of his supposed nuclear programs was a lie. Everything went into the immortality vial. If he finds the key to create it on a mass scale, he will create vials for his entire military." Bob said

All was quiet in the room and Richard went into deep thought.

"Do you understand, he can create a military that cannot die? They will be immortal." Bo said.

"If he lives forever, how am I going to stop him?" Richard said.

"Yes he is immortal, however, if you can cut off his head he'll die. There must be a connection between the brain and the heart for it to work. But he will live forever and millions of crazy, radical soldiers will live forever. In war he may only lose 5 percent of his soldiers and still conquer the whole world. Even a nuclear blast won't kill them all unless their heads were blown completely off" Bob said.

"What's in it for me?" Richard asked.

A piece of paper was slid across the table.

Richard looked down and his jaw dropped. Before him was a check for one hundred million dollars.

"You do this, I'll sign the check for you to cash to give to your family. Tax free. Most importantly you will be the first to receive a vial when we figure out how to create it."

Richard was sweating bullets. He went through customs at the North Korean airport. Here he was with truly nothing but a suitcase with clothes and another with magic tricks. Oh yeah, there was that special deck of cards.

Hands were all over him feeling for anything illegal. It was very invasive and uncomfortable.

"Hey man, you going to buy me dinner first? Richard said.

The customs official did not crack a smile.

Next came the inspection of his luggage.

This customs official was not gentle with his belongings.

"Hey man be careful, you don't want to make your great leader mad if something in here breaks and I can't perform," Richard said.

The official pulled out the multiple packs of cards. All were the same and all were sealed. He randomly opened one up and starting flipping the cards.

"Geeze man, I can't do my tricks if you are going to ruin the cards." Richard said.

Again no reaction from the official but Richard was about to explode in panic. The customs agent was reaching for the deadly pack.

"Hey, do me a favor and hurry up. You know I'm performing for your leader tonight and I need to get to the hotel and rest up. You don't want me screwing up a trick because I'm tired and making the Great Leader mad do you? If he asks why I messed up I'll be sure to give him your name."

The official threw the unopened deadly pack down into the luggage.

"You may pass."

It was a small affair. Magician after magician delighted Huan Juan. Richard's blood boiled. How could that fat little dude be having such a good time after all the people he had killed?

Because Richard was a magician he was a man of

details. He could see what he presumed was the case that contained the one and only immortal serum vial left on planet earth.

It was being treated like the nuclear launch code suitcase, usually called the football, which followed the President of the U.S. on his trips.

Richard took to the stage. He did some impressive sleight of hand tricks that earned him the applause of the great leader.

It was time for the target throwing trick.

"Ladies and Gentlemen. I will show you an incredible card trick."

Some of the stage hands set up targets around the stage. There was a candle where he threw the card and snuffed out the flame.

The next trick was books set up where he could throw cards between them with only millimeters separating them.

Again his skill was applauded.

It was time. Richard reached into his bag for the deadly pack.

"Ladies and Gentlemen, I will now demonstrate how I can throw a card and have it end up in your shirt or jacket pocket."

The crowd applauded yet again.

Richard carefully opened the pack and drew out

the deadly cards.

Of course, the three of spades would turn up as the top card. The same card he had cut himself on just a few weeks ago.

Huan Juan was about twenty feet away from him. An easy hit.

Richard didn't know if he would make it out alive or not but he had to try.

He drew his hand back and with a hard flip the three of spades flew through the air. It was dead on. The great leader eyes lit up in shock. Then his hand went to his throat. It was just a brief second. Then his head tilted back and fell off.

Richard had done it.

The Great Leader's security team jumped into action. They were in shock at first but Richard was ready for this performance of a life time.

Flick, flick, flick. The cards flew out of his hands and each one killed a different security officer.

Bodies fell everywhere. People screamed and ran out of the room.

Flick, flick, flick. Richard knew he had less than 52 chances to stop anyone in security from coming at him. He was so good he could throw and kill just by seeing someone out of the corner of his eye.

His focus was on the immortal vial that waited in

the small briefcase. He knew he must reach it. He now heard the unmistakable thump of helicopters overhead. He knew it was the CIA coming in to support him. The room was clear. Bodies laid everywhere.

Richard reached down to the brief case. He never heard the bullet that entered his stomach. The pain was unbelievable.

He was going to die not from the tumor but a gunshot. Blood poured out of his stomach. Richard saw the second North Korean security team coming in through the door. He grabbed the briefcase and popped it open. He could not believe it was unlocked.

There before him was his only chance. The beautiful Immortal Vial.

Another bullet entered his shoulder.

Gunfire could be heard coming from the hallways. Richard was fading into blackness.

The vial was in his hand. If he could just bring the liquid to his lips. Maybe, just maybe, it would not be too late.

Suddenly his hand was ripped from near his face. That vial was so close.

A man with a crew cut and who was obviously U.S. military of some sort took the vial from his hand.

"I don't think so, magic boy."

"Please, I'm dying."

The man pulled his sidearm from his side and put it up to Richards head.

I wonder if I'll get a Star on the memorial wall?

CHANGING GEARS

A. B. ALVAREZ

Who doesn't like a hot cup of joe in the morning Handmade. Responsibly sourced. And when trouble strikes, isn't it good to know that your friendly neighborhood barista has it all well in hand?

So let me start by reassuring everyone that Shannon did not die. I think its important to make that known up front as the death of a friend or loved one can sometimes jar the senses and that is not part of my approved programming.

Of course, Shannon did die, but not for very long. I, on the other hand, died a long time ago, but managed to get past that with little change or emotional consequence to the world.

The coffee shop I worked in was what you would expect: dark wood grain everywhere you looked (most of it fake) and counters, chairs, and tables where people paid for the privilege to consume various quantities of caffeine.

The lighting in the morning, my favorite, through the large picture windows at the front of the store, let in the most beautiful yellow sun you can imagine. Even the patrons, looking dazed and alert in alternating sequences, looked like something from a properly designed movie set where the unsuspecting townspeople were suddenly surprised with the end of the world. I noticed a playing card on one of the tables. The three of diamonds.

I stood in my green apron and stared my stare at the next patron. "Good morning," I said. I always tried to translate the day into words for the customer to feel maybe a little something extra to start their day.

"I'll have a double shot cappuccino, with a little caramel, sugar, half-and-half with a splash of almond milk, and two extra hits of chocolate syrup," the young lady said. "Also, make sure the almond milk is extra hot, and add four pumps of diet hazelnut." I love it when a customer comes up with something complex rather than the usual cup-of-regular-coffee-with-milk-please though usually without the please.

As a barista drone there wasn't much I could do except listen to the orders, programming them into the coffee machine (which could handle about a million combinations of ingredients; okay maybe a few hundred thousand), and would get it right every time. Since I was responsible for programming it I felt a responsibility. I love feeling responsible.

At some point, after handling a few dozen happy and not so happy customers She came in.

Shannon.

Now Shannon was a regular. Not a regular regular. More like a decaf regular. Nothing disturbed her, and I made sure to keep her going as she put in her order. She was also an order of magnitude prettier than the other baristas I worked with (it does get tiring seeing the same dronish faces everyday) and I wondered if someone like her, a customer, couldn't be lucky enough to work along side us, a bunch of programmed drones with just enough deep learning to appreciate what was going on around us, but not caring much about leaving. I mean, really, is there a better job than that of serving coffee to truly appreciative people day in and day out? Knowing that you touched so many lives so many times per day?

I had my tribe. I loved my tribe. Well, maybe not loved, perhaps only tolerated, but they were my people, so to speak. The only thing I could think of doing was being with them all the time and just enjoy the luck I had to have been part of their group when we were brought in to work at this coffee shop in the middle of the most incredible block anywhere.

I looked at Shannon and wished I could find the words to ask her to join us. Of course, I don't have the words available in my vocabulary so I said the next best thing: "Good morning, Shannon. The usual?"

She smiled. What a beautiful smile. It matched the sunlight. It made me think of freshly brewed Columbian roast with just a hint of hazelnut. Her hair glinted as just a bit of light bounced off her freshly washed hair and entered my visual sensor making me feel a little lighter and yet grounded. What must it be like to not have the joy I felt standing here behind the counter? Would she one day be able to appreciate all that I felt and the happiness I still feel at serving her and her compatriots? Especially serving her?

The next thing I knew her eyes were rolling back,

her shoulders slumped and she slowly fell to the ground. My flash memory sent a non-maskable interrupt: first aid was warranted. I ran as fast as I could, this was obviously an emergency that needed to be taken care before the breakfast sandwiches were done, and I was around the counter, first passing the coffee brewer, the pastries, the three ovens, and the door into the kitchen area which was really more a storage room for all of the things that have to be stored that will eventually make their way out to the counter and showcase.

A crowd of people had formed around her. Shannon's head was at an odd angle, but I took that as a good sign. A young man knelt by her side and began to put something under her head, probably to make her comfortable. I touched his shoulder and he suddenly jumped away. "Don't worry. I've got this."

The crowd, apparently surprised at the speed with which I was reacting took a step back. I felt good. I knew this was something I could do.

I placed my finger sensor against the inside of her throat just below her jaw where the neck and her skull met. The pulse was weak. I wasn't sure what had occurred to her health, but she was experiencing a minor loss of consciousness. I held her hand and felt for a pulse on her wrist. Again, very weak.

"Please call 911," I said. I looked at another young woman whose face was a collection of wide-eyes, open mouth and pale skin. I knew that she was both in awe at my abilities to handle the situation and that I was able to say more than just Good morning.

Behind the counter I heard Angelica say, "Everyone remain calm. The police and ambulance are on their way." Angelica started soon after me at the coffee shop. When I look at her I know I can rely on her no matter what the problem: straws are out, more cups need to be pulled out of the kitchen-but-really-the-storage-room, and to make a great cup of coffee.

I still held Shannon's wrist when I saw her entire body sag in an obviously dangerous way. I placed the palm of my hand on her chest (and by chest I mean directly above her bra and before her suprasternal notch so as not to inappropriately touch her and risk offending a repeat customer).

Her heart did not appear to be moving. I snapped the buttons off her blouse and began CPR. I counted in my head as, again, I did not have the vocabulary to vocalize what I was doing. One, two, three. I pushed down on her chest. I felt her pulse. Still nothing. This was not progressing in the direction I preferred this to go. Once again, I compressed her sternum, this time having to push down on the center of her chest thereby touching her breasts which I was recording so as to prove that I did not touch her without a legally valid reason.

I checked her pulse. There did not appear to be one. I reached around her forehead and touched her left and right temple where her hair did not grow. The readings were not encouraging. Her brainwave activity was quite disturbing and I knew that it was time for a more extreme, and yet pleasant (for me), approach.

I stood, turned and went into the store room. Carrying out a spare model, I placed the brand new personnel carrier on the ground directly to her right. The patrons happily stepped away from her and from me. Their eyes opened wide in what I knew was delight. Almost envy.

One gentlemen made a sound about not knowing what I was doing, but I simply touched his shoulder and he jumped away as well. It was always such a pleasure to deal with such understanding.

I felt for a pulse again. Her eyes not registering. Her heart not beating. No pulse. I could feel the concern in my system rising as I knew the risk to her rose steadily. What I did next was the most important step of all.

I turned her over. Quite an achievement given her prone state on the floor.

I tore open her top to reveal her back. Her skin was smooth and uninterrupted except for her bra strap. I pop open the bra snap.

I extended the claws from my hand and dug them into her back and pulled down to reveal her bloody backbone. I heard screams in front of me. The customers were concerned for our welfare. I was moved.

I grabbed her spinal column and gripped it tight enough to crush it.

I felt the spinal fluid running over my hand because I felt a slight short in between my joints. She was going to be overwhelmed with joy.

Her nerve endings fired off tiny little electrical impulses I sensed, no felt, through the mesh embedded in the palm my hand. The flow of her life entered the tips of my fingers. Her mind downloaded into my cache.

She never moved. Once I had embraced her spinal cord all movement had stopped. The download proceeded. I thought I heard sounds like yelling or screaming or maybe sounds of happiness and ecstasy.

It stopped. I released her and the cord hung

outside of her back like the handle of a bag or a suitcase.

I wiped my hand on my green apron. The wetness puzzled me. While I didn't want my hand to be too dry I also knew that I had to conduct at least a marginal amount. I turned to the drone laying face-up on the floor next to Shannon's discarded form.

The burnished brushed steel chest opened like the petals of a flower and allowed my hand to enter and make the final connection. I wondered, the few times I wondered, what it would feel like to feel Shannon. To have her mind as part of mine. To feel as her mind uploaded and totally engulfed who I was and became more complete with her and then to feel as she would drain away. Slowly. Completely.

I would put in a change order to describe the efficiency of a new transfer method.

My hand retracted automatically from the drone and the flower that was her chest closed within a few seconds.

For a time we were together. Apart, yet together. Separate, but equal.

Shannon sat up. Her vocabulary was limited, as mine was, and her one eyed head swiveled. I stood and I gave her a hand up. The doors opened and a few new customers came in; two pushed a gurney toward the empty shell of my former customer.

Former, because she left her body.

Current, because now she was on our side. I knew that she would enjoy her new surroundings as I do.

As we all do.

I returned to my place behind the counter at the register where our customers pay while they wait for the cup of joe only I could make them.

Shannon stood by the coffee machine.

THE KILLING POOL

SERENA B. MILLER

Everyone needs a sanctuary from time to time. Even a ten-year-old killer.

"Get lost, kid," Jackson said, with disgust. "And clean yourself up before your mom gets home."

Cherie stumbled out of the bedroom as her mother's latest boyfriend turned over in bed and went to sleep. At twelve, she wasn't entirely certain what had just happened, but it had been painful, humiliating, and terrifying.

Get cleaned up? She didn't need to be told. She wanted to run to the shower and stand under the hot spray forever and ever until she could feel clean again —if that were even possible. But that would have to wait. She was afraid to stay in the house alone with him long enough to do anything except throw some things into her backpack and run.

She did not know Jackson well. He had not been part of their life for very long. She had thought him friendly enough when her mother first brought him home, but now she realized his friendliness had hidden a darker purpose.

Who knew what might happen in the six hours before her mother would come back? She had no intention of finding out.

With tears streaming down her face, she silently crept into her bedroom, locked the door, and changed her clothes from the skin out. It was hard to look at her underwear. Ashamed, she buried her soiled panties deep beneath the dirty clothes in her hamper, wishing she could burn them. Perhaps later. When it was safe.

She emptied her pink school backpack on the bed and randomly shoved an extra outfit into the pack. Then she chose two favorite books to take with her. Always books. She knew she'd need the escape they provided to help keep the memories of what had just happened to her at bay. Holding her backpack in one hand, she opened the door of her bedroom and listened. Was that Jackson moving around? Should she crawl out the window to get away? To her relief, she heard him snoring in her mother's room.

She crept into the kitchen pantry and quietly began to pull food off the shelves. There wasn't much to choose from. Some tuna. A small box of crackers. Cheese. A bag of strawberry Twizzlers. Two bottles of water. A few other things. She hefted her backpack. Yes, that was enough.

At was then, the full impact of what she had been through hit and she began to shake. Even though it was late spring and not at all cold in the house, she pulled her mother's warmest coat out of the closet. It was a puffy, silky coat, light blue, and she zipped it all the way up to her chin. It was laughably large on her, but being enveloped in it comforted her. She knew that her mother would never have allowed Jackson in the house if she had known. Her mother would have protected her. The shaking began to diminish.

She sat the backpack beside the kitchen door, ready to grab, and took a long, hard, look at her mother's bedroom door. Jackson was snoring so loudly it felt like those snores might tear apart their flimsy house. Cherie was only twelve, but there was something she intended to take care of before she went away.

There were gloves in her mother's coat, left there from the winter months. Cherie pulled them on. Then she crossed the room to a row of cabinets, stood on her tiptoes, and felt around for the handgun her mother always kept loaded and ready for that intruder she was forever fearful of breaking in. She had taught Cherie, frequently left at home by herself, how to point and shoot it if necessary.

It was ironic that when her mother had left for work this morning, she had expressed relief that Jackson, so big and strong, would be there to protect her.

The gun felt heavy in her hand, but it took little effort for her to slip through the bedroom door. Jackson has shifted positions in his sleep. He now lay spread-eagled on his back, naked, his mouth hanging open, drooling, sound asleep.

Her mother worked two jobs, so in addition to books and homework, Cherie entertained herself with her computer and television several hours a day. Recently, she had developed interest in a crime-related television series. That was why she understood the need for gloves to hide fingerprints and powder residue, and how her mother had to have an iron-clad alibi. If Cherie did this, right now, the other waitresses and customers at the busy diner would easily be able to vouch for her mother.

Very deliberately she walked to the bed, pointed the mouth of the gun into her tormentor's open mouth and pulled the trigger. The bullet blew off the top of Jackson's head.

He jerked, but he didn't so much as open his eyes. Cherie was afraid he had not felt anything, which made her mad. She wanted him to feel something, so at point blank range she shot him in the chest, in the stomach, and between the legs. On the fifth shot, she missed. The bullet tore into the mattress. She had begun to cry and the tears had blurred her vision. . She forced herself to stop crying, wiped her eyes and took stock. Satisfied that he would never hurt anyone again, she walked back into the kitchen and carefully placed the gun in the sink. There were blood splatters on the gun. It would need to be cleaned. The sink was a good place to leave it.

The shaking had stopped entirely now. A deep calm stole over her. She was no longer afraid of taking a long hot shower. Her mother wouldn't be home anytime soon. They lived far enough out that there was no one to hear the gunshot. She had time. She had plenty of time to shower, change into fresh clothes, and walk out the door. But she had also seen enough TV to know that unforeseen complications often happened. Bloody clothes were found. People showed up at the wrong time.

They lived at the edge of a national forest comprised of thousands of wilderness acres. The woods behind her house were deep and dark and had many secret places that she had discovered. A little girl with a mother always at work had time and freedom to explore, which she did often even though her mother told her to stay in the house with the doors locked when she was away.

Although she felt no regret in killing Jackson, she did regret having soiled her home with his ugly body. Until it was found and removed, she intended to stay far away. Neither she nor her mother liked living in a dirty house. From the time she was little, she had liked for things to be neat and clean. It bothered her that something so dirty was still lying in her mother's bedroom.

There was a place she liked. About a mile in. A small cave. Just an indentation really, but big enough for a young girl to stay hidden for a few hours until someone discovered Jackson's body and took it away. It might also be a good place to stash the blood-splattered coat. Her mother would not like what had happened to her coat.

The cave was exactly as she had left it the last time she had been there. That time, she had spent a day clearing out most of the rocks and pebbles so they wouldn't jab her when she sat down. Because rain never touched it, the floor of the cave was permanently dry and dusty. It felt velvety and welcome to her. As she sat with her legs dangling over the lip of the cave, she could see far down to the creek bed below. It was a lovely view.

She stashed her bits of food away on a rock ledge and rolled out her sleeping bag. She had pretty much held herself together for the past hour it took to deal with things and get to the cave, but now that she was safe and hidden, she gave herself permission to fall apart completely. She waited, and waited, but she didn't fall apart. Instead, she sat and processed as wave after wave of disgusting memories rushed through her mind.

Then she shook herself, and focused on how it had felt when she pulled the trigger and ended Jackson's life. This memory made her smile. She sat still for a long time and savored every detail.

Feeling slightly better, she grabbed the package of Twizzlers, ate two of them, and then rummaged around in her backpack for the deck of playing cards she had brought. Her mom had taught her how to play solitaire only last week. This should make the time go faster. She could not go home until the police had sorted things out.

As she laid the cards down, one by one, keeping them in a straight, evenly spaced line-she realized she had never been in the cave this late in the afternoon before. The light was different.

Red queen on black king. Black Jack on queen. Red ten on Jack. She turned the deck over and started again, dealing in threes. An ace of diamonds was the first card to turn up.

The afternoon sun became even more interesting as it slanted in at an ever-changing angle. It illuminated the ceiling and walls in ways she'd never seen before.

She moved the ace to above the line of cards. A two of diamonds appeared. That was fantastic. Now, if she moved it to the ace…

A slash of sunlight blinded her for a moment and she quickly turned her head, protecting her eyes. When she could see again, the sun had set, and only a small wedge of it was visible against the cave wall. A very specific slice of the cave wall.

For a moment, she thought she was seeing things.

Then she stood and peered closer. There, painted in what might have been some sort of animal, or perhaps human, blood, was the drawing of a woman in front of what looked to be a door. The woman was not like anyone Cherie had ever seen before. She was short, and squat, and had pendulous breasts. She appeared to be pushing at a door. The drawing was primitive and even at Cherie's age, she thought she could draw better.

The painting looked like it might have been done of this particular cave, except for one difference— that opening pictured in the back.

Cherie knew that there was no such opening. She had been all over the small cave. It was only a few square feet. But the picture intrigued her. She went to the back of the cave yet once again and examined it. As the sun sank lower, she saw that there were, indeed, some fissures in the smooth rock wall that could possibly be a door. Carefully, she pushed on it, and the wall moved slightly. She pushed harder, and it moved again. This time she put her shoulder into it and shoved, and a gaping hole appeared where a rock wall had been.

One of the other things Cherie had packed was a good flashlight because she suspected she would not be coming home tonight. She retrieved it from her pack and flicked it on. What she saw when she stepped into the cave was astonishing. There were well-worn stairs that led down to a large pool. The water was crystal clear, and there appeared to be seats chiseled out around the edge, just beneath the surface of the water.

Mesmerized by her discovery, Cherie approached the pool. Unlike the outer small cave, the ceiling of this opening was so very high she could not see the top. The place echoed with her footsteps.

She played her flashlight around the walls and saw that nearly every inch was covered with elaborate paintings. All of women. All of women taking care of other women. Bringing one another food, covering one another with tapestries. There were varying degrees of mastery so it was obvious the paintings had been done by different artists, but all were of women ministering to other women.

The paintings were interesting, but it was the water that drew her. It felt magnetic, and the pull was strong. She walked toward it and discovered that it wasn't just her flashlight illuminating the water, but there was a glow coming from within. She turned off the flashlight and could still see in the darkness. The glow from the water illuminated the cave in a magical way.

She placed her flashlight on one of the stone benches and gave into the desire to soak herself in this lovely water. Marveling at what was happening, she removed all her clothing and stepped in. The water was only slightly cooler than her own body temperature and it had a delicious texture to it. It felt as though it had been thickened with something silky. It reminded her of the aloe vera her mother sometimes used on cuts and burns. The feeling was soothing.

As she allowed herself to sink deeper into the liquid, she felt a slightly tingling sensation wherever it touched her skin. Once she was submerged up to her chin, she found that she had no desire to get out. The liquid surrounded her with warmth and comfort. Even the pain that Jackson had left within her body began to lessen. It was as though the water was deliberately healing the tears and bruises he had left.

She now saw the reason for the curved benches just below the surface. They made it possible to recline in the water, and as the liquid soothed her small body, she discovered that she did not care if she ever left.

Her mind hung suspended for a long time. She did not want to figure this out. She did not want to try to rationalize this amazing experience away.

Although she knew it was impossible, it began to feel as though the pool was healing her mind as well.

After a long, long time, she was aware of a presence. Something was within the cave with her and, surprisingly, that knowledge was not disturbing. When she opened her eyes she couldn't see anything at first. Then she noticed a sort of fog in a shape of a woman, a whirl of air that shifted and moved and shimmered and danced in front of her. There might have been the shape of a face, but she wasn't sure.

"Who are you?" she asked. "What are you?"

The cave air grew slightly colder as the presence settled down upon her. A mist, a fog, but oddly refreshing.

"I am the mistress of the killing pool," the mist whispered.

"I don't understand," Cherie said.

"You have come to the outer cave often?"

"I have."

"And today you came here looking for solace? You came because you were upset?"

"Yes."

"That is why the opening to the pool revealed itself. The pool only accepts and heals those females who have endured your particular kind of pain. Do you feel better now?"

"A little."

"Then you must come out of the pool and dress."

"I am wet," Cherie said. "And I have no towel."

"You will not need one," the mist said.

Cherie rose from the pool, and the liquid sluiced off her, leaving her as dry as before she went in. There wasn't even a chill from air on her skin such as water left. She felt comfortable and warm in the softly illuminated cave as she dressed herself, but she left her mother's coat lying on the bench.

"You don't want the coat?" the mist asked.

"Not anymore."

"Why."

"It's...bloody."

"The blood on your mother's coat calls out to me. He was a bad man?" the mist asked.

"How did you know..."

"He is dead now?" the mist asked.

"Yes."

"Oh, good girl!" the mist exclaimed. "The pool and I are very pleased. Now, follow me."

There was an opening that led into a sort of bed chamber. The headboard of the bed was made of crystal, the rug beneath her feet made of the greenest moss she had ever seen.

"What is this place?" Cherie asked.

"Your new home."

"But I have a home," Cherie said

"Doesn't it have a man's dead body in it?"

"Yes, but the police will come and take him away," Cherie reasoned. "When I go home it will just be my mother and me again."

"There will be others," the mist said. "Your mother is loving, but she is also weak and needy. Other men will come. You will be safer here."

"But I love my mom," Cherie said. "How long do I have to stay?"

"Until you wish to leave," the mist said. "But remember—there is peace here, and freedom from fear."

"How did this place get here?" Cherie asked.

"It was created by a tribe of ancient women who knew it would be needed."

"Did the things that happened to me happen to the women who built it?" Cherie asked.

"Yes, and they also responded by taking a life. Killing was hard for them because women are created to give life and nurture, not to harm. There was one woman who had a particular kind of magic. She used up every bit of it to create this place for herself and for others. Now—you need to rest and heal awhile longer, little one."

Cherie obeyed the mist. She rested. She slept in the beautiful soft bed with the crystal headboard. She floated in the pool. Time evaporated as she read not only her own books, but those left behind by other girls and women. Some of the books were very ancient. Some were relatively new. Some were notebooks written by the women who had spent time here.

And then there were the names written on the wall. Too many to count. She found that she was growing tired of the weight of knowing the stories of the women who had come here.

"It is time for me to leave now," Cherie did not know how long she had been in the cave, and she had lost count of the times she had gone into the pool. "My mother is going to be frightened and wondering where I am."

"Things will be different for you now," the mist said. "You will be stronger. But if you are ever again need us, you will always be welcome here."

Cherie did not have to push on the door. It opened on its own. As she walked out into the sunshine, the mist whispered one last thing.

"Always remember. Women were made to nurture, not to harm."

The rock door slowly closed behind her, she

noticed that her pink backpack and her bits of food were gone, as was her sleeping bag.

Cherie walked back through the woods feeling significantly stronger than when she had come this way earlier. How long had she been here? Had her mother been worried?

When she arrived, her mother was distraught.

"Where have you been?" Her mother grabbed her like she would never let her go. "We looked everywhere for you. The whole community looked for you. We were afraid that whoever killed Jackson had also taken you. What happened to you?"

"Nothing," Cherie said. "I went for a walk in the woods. There is a cave. I fell asleep there."

The police came. They questioned her carefully, over and over, until her mother asked them to stop. Cherie's answers were always the same. She went for a walk, there was a cave, and she fell asleep. Jackson's murder remained a great mystery. Cherie's mother was deeply grateful that her daughter had taken a walk that day and had not been in the house when the gruesome murder took place.

About six months later, her mother brought a new man home. They had been dating. Her mother said he needed a place to stay for a while.

Cherie was playing a video game. This was the first time she had met the new boyfriend.

"Hello," she said, not taking her eyes off the game.

"Hi," he said.

"Freddie loves children," her mother said. "Isn't that right, Freddie?"

Cherie glanced up from her game and met the new boyfriend's eyes. He smiled. She had seen that expression before. Her mother must be blind. Boyfriend Freddie was a predator who apparently liked young girls. She could feel his eyes appraising her.

She found herself smiling back at him in anticipation. She had missed the killing pool. It would be nice to go back.

ABOUT THE AUTHORS

A. B. Alvarez was born and raised in New York and found he couldn't keep his love of the city out of his first published series. Every book in the series either takes place in New York, or has  New York characters who bring a a fresh perspective to a story of loss, revenge, and ultimately of closure. He is already working feverishly on his next series. lk.ljemory.com/ABAlvarez

 **Serena B. Miller** is an award-winning, best-selling author who has written multiple romances about the large Amish population living near her in Ohio. Two made-for-TV movies, *An Uncommon Grace* and *Love Finds You in*

Sugarcreek, have been based on her novels. Serena also writes historical and contemporary fiction and is presently working on a line of cozy mysteries: *The Secrets of Sugarcreek*. serenabmiller.com

---

Derek E. Miller spent five years as a military contractor in the war zone of Afghanistan. The experience left him with friends all  over the world, an appreciation for our men and women in the military, and an uncontrollable desire to hit the ground whenever fireworks go off. It also gave him a desire to channel some of his experience into writing YA novels. His diary series, *The Attic Diary*, *The Kamikaze Diary*, and *The Ghost Army Diary* was the result. He also has a popular how-to book entitled: *Military Contractor's Handbook: How to get Hired... and Survive*. derekemiller.com

---

Jesse R. Lyle wears many hats as he runs a computer tech consulting and repair business. He backed into writing short fiction after he and his

D&D buddies' campaigns started drifting into real life. However, the thrill of building Dungeon scenarios gave him a taste for creating new universes and odd characters. This anthology is his first foray into the world of published short stories. jesserlyle.com

ALSO BY A. B. ALVAREZ

THE KIDNAPPING ANNA TRILOGY

- *Kidnapping Anna (Book 1)*
- *ADX Florence (Book 2)*
- *The Montague Tubes (Book 3)*

ALSO BY SERENA B. MILLER

LOVE'S JOURNEY IN SUGARCREEK SERIES

- *Love's Journey in Sugarcreek: The Sugar Haus Inn (Book 1)*
- *Love's Journey in Sugarcreek: Rachel's Rescue (Book 2)*
- *Love's Journey in Sugarcreek: Love Rekindled (Book 3)*

LOVE'S JOURNEY ON MANITOULIN ISLAND SERIES

- *Love's Journey on Manitoulin Island: Moriah's Lighthouse (Book 1)*
- *Love's Journey on Manitoulin Island: Moriah's Fortress (Book 2)*
- *Love's Journey on Manitoulin Island: Moriah's Stronghold (Book 3)*
- *Love's Journey on Manitoulin Island: Eliza's Lighthouse (Book 4)*

MICHIGAN NORTHWOODS HISTORICAL ROMANCE

- *The Measure of Katie Calloway (Book 1)*
- *Under a Blackberry Moon (Book 2)*
- *A Promise to Love (Book 3)*

UNCOMMON GRACE SERIES

- *An Uncommon Grace (Book 1)*
- *Hidden Mercies (Book 2)*
- *Fearless Hope (Book 3)*

THE DOREEN SIZEMORE ADVENTURES

- *Murder On The Texas Eagle (Book 1)*
- *Murder At The Buckstaff Bathhouse (Book 2)*
- *Murder At Slippery Slop Youth Camp (Book 3)*
- *Murder On The Mississippi Queen (Book 4)*
- *Murder On The Mystery Mansion (Book 5)*
- *The Accidental Adventures of Doreen Sizemore (5 Book Collection)*

UNCATEGORIZED

- *A Way of Escape*
- *More Than Happy: The Wisdom of Amish Parenting*

ALSO BY DEREK E. MILLER

THE DIARY SERIES

- *The Attic Diary*
- *The Kamikaze Diary*
- *The Ghost Army Diary*

AN ESPRESSO SHORT SERIES

- *Third Monkey*
- *Alien Pet*

NON-FICTION

- *Military Contractor's Handbook: How to get Hired… and Survive*